Evan

Kiss Me Again, Cowboy

Sweet Grass Ranch
Book 2

Maddie James

Evan: Kiss Me Again, Cowboy

Sweet Grass Ranch, Book 2

Maddie James

Evan: Kiss Me Again, Cowboy
Sweet Grass Ranch, Book 2

Evan MacKay is grateful to have his four brothers working beside him at Sweet Grass Ranch. Maintaining their ranch lifestyle is his priority, but the bank breathing down his neck and he worries the ranch can't support their growing family. Secretly, he waits for the other boot to drop.

Turns out the other boots are Jimmy Choo black stilettos worn by the new bank loan manager.

Jessica Chase doesn't claim to be an expert on ranching, but she's a whiz in finance, particularly in whipping delinquent accounts into shape. As the new kid on the block, she is driven to succeed, and ready to pull the Sweet Grass Ranch account back into solvency. She is also eager to rebuild her life in South Dakota.

The city woman in heels knows a lot about money, Evan admits, but nothing about cattle. He tries to advise her about ranch business, but she dismisses his recommendations. While intrigued by the abrupt rancher who tries to educate her about cows, Jessica feels her resolve slipping. She has a job to do, and it doesn't involve kissing the grumpy cowboy.

But kiss him, she does.

Can Jessica rein in her growing attraction for Evan while remaining committed to her professional goal? Will love triumph over the bottom line?

Chapter One

Evan MacKay eased in a breath, crisp morning air filling his lungs. The aroma of sweet prairie grass, still damp with dew, tangled with the acrid smell of wood smoke drifting up from the bunkhouse chimney. A hawk soared lazily overhead, riding a warm updraft, searching for prey.

The combined effects signaled both comfort and home.

Shifting in the saddle, his gaze rolled over the South Dakota hills dotted with cattle. *Sweet Grass Ranch.* Fences crisscrossed the landscape, the sturdy barricades protecting the herds. So much had changed since his father had passed, but the ranch lands and the hills remained steadfast.

A familiar ache landed across his chest—a hollow sense of loss settled into his bones. He wasn't sure he would ever be free of it.

"We will get this right, Dad," he murmured. "I'm not giving up on this land or our family."

His buckskin quarter horse flicked back his ears at his words. Evan stroked his neck, taking comfort in the solid warmth of his sturdy body.

He would hold the ranch together through sheer grit if he

had to. Failure was not an option. The bank could threaten all they wanted, but he aimed to keep Sweet Grass Ranch in the family, as it had been for generations.

Evan set his jaw, his resolve blazing with determination as he turned the horse toward home. The sun had crested the hills, spilling light into the day. A spattering of color blanketed the hills—fall was landing early this year. They'd have to move cattle down before long.

No matter what storms raged around him—or inside him—the ranch work continued. And Evan aimed to see it remain for a long time.

The barn doors creaked open as he led the gelding inside. The rich and earthy smells of hay and leather enveloped him. He nodded to Aiden and Aaron, his brothers, as the youngest MacKay twins mucked out the stalls.

"Morning, boss," Aiden said, leaning on his pitchfork.

Evan tipped his hat. "You boys sleep alright?"

"Well as can be," Aaron said. "Back's a mite sore, though."

"That's what happens when you try riding Tornado bareback." Aiden elbowed his brother with a grin.

Aaron shoved him good-naturedly. Evan hid a smile. The twins' playful banter never failed to lift his spirits. He envied their youthful enthusiasm. Other times, he wanted them to pull their own weight.

"Well, you two need to get off the circuit soon. The deal was no rodeo until the ranch was back on its feet. You've slipped into some bad habits lately." He eyed his younger brothers.

Aiden coughed and glanced at Aaron. "We were planning to leave out tonight for Denver. Are you saying we need to cancel?"

The younger brothers exchanged worried glances.

Evan sighed and shook his head. "No. Do this one, then no

more. You got that? We need you here. A lot to do before the snow comes."

Aaron saluted. "Yes, boss."

Evan jerked back. "That's enough of that boss shit. You got that? Now get to work."

The younger twins snickered and returned to their mucking.

After tending to the buckskin, Evan headed outside where several ranch hands had gathered. Connor tipped his hat in greeting. "What's the plan today, Evan?"

"Same as yesterday," he said. "You boys know the drill. Take your crew and start mending that stretch of fence in the east pasture. Jackson, you and your guys are feeding." He turned away, then halted, looking back. "And don't forget we've got vaccinations coming up. We need to get ready for all that."

Conner nodded. "Yes, sir."

The men headed to their tasks with quiet competence. Evan watched them work, pride swelling in his chest. He knew each hand by name, their families, and their troubles. These men had been with the ranch for years, loyal through the best and worst of times. Together, they would weather this storm, too.

He made his way to the pasture just south of the house, boots crunching on the gravel path. They kept the pregnant cows and new babies there, closer to the house and barns during the colder months. The morning air whipped around a group of outbuildings and hinted at the coming winter chill.

He inspected the fence line, testing each post along the way. Rotten wood crumbled under his grip. Barbed wire sagged between posts, rusted and frayed. This stretch clearly needed mending.

"Dammit." *Didn't we just repair this section a year ago?*

Evan kneeled and examined a broken post more closely. Dry rot had weakened the wood over seasons of sun and rain.

He sighed, tallying the repairs in his head. Lumber, wire, staples —it would all add up fast.

They might have mended the wiring, but this wood had been in the ground for a long time. The entire section might need to be replaced.

The costs were mounting, but what choice did he have? Letting the fences fall into disrepair was unthinkable. If the livestock got loose, it'd be a disaster. Keeping the cows and calves safe and secure over the winter and spring was a priority.

Evan stood, rolling his shoulders against the familiar ache. He took in the sweeping vista of the ranch, the only home he'd ever known. From the main house where he and his brothers lived, to the weathered barns, and to the rolling hills fading into the distance, he loved every inch of this land. His gaze traveled up the hill to his mom's cabin, the one his dad had built for her a few years before he died. He would fight to his last breath to protect all of it.

With that thought steeling his resolve, Evan headed back to start the day's work. There were animals to feed, repairs to be made. That afternoon, he had to go over the financials with his brother, Ethan and sister-in-law, Brandley. No time for doubt or second-guessing. Sweet Grass needed him.

Needed them all if it was going to survive. As much as he wished he could, he couldn't do it alone.

* * *

His twin brother, Ethan, turned away from the coffeemaker as Evan entered the kitchen.

"Morning," Ethan said. "You were up early. Coffee?" He tipped a mug his way.

"Yes. Thanks." Evan took the full mug. "Fences need mending down south. Posts rotting out."

Ethan poured a second mug of coffee for himself, his expression clouded with concern. "Again? Didn't we replace that entire section last year?" He took a sip.

"That's what I thought, too. Looks like we mended wire but not posts. We need new posts."

Ethan stood and appeared to be thinking, as if that explanation didn't sit well. "What's it going to run us?"

"Too much," Evan grunted. "Lumber's gone up and the hardware store just raised prices. We'll be patching as we can."

He left the rest unsaid between them—money was dwindling fast. While they thought they'd had a solid plan to dig their way out of the mess left when their father died, the ranch was sinking deeper into debt. But Evan wouldn't speak of it, not yet. Ethan knew well enough without him spelling it out.

"We'll manage somehow," Ethan said firmly. "Always have. When's Dylan coming back from Montana?"

Evan looked away, jaw tightening. Manage how? The numbers were clear, and they weren't good. But voicing his doubts felt like admitting defeat.

"Evan?"

"What?"

"Dylan?"

"Oh. I think he's gone another week." Dylan, their middle brother, was a Deputy Sheriff for Meade County. "I believe he said his training lasted that long."

"In Billings, right?"

"I believe so."

"Hmmm. Close to the Rankin's."

"Yes. I suppose." Evan wasn't sure what his brother was getting at—their sister, Sarah, lived close to the Rankins at Rock Creek Ranch, so maybe that was it—but at the moment, he wasn't in the mood to figure it out. He had other things on his mind.

Like he was failing his father, failing the legacy entrusted to him—a legacy generations deep, and rooted in their land. The thought hollowed him out inside.

Ethan clasped his shoulder. "Look. We're in this together, remember? This burden is not solely on your shoulders."

Evan managed a terse nod. Ethan meant well, and he appreciated his brother's steady presence. Evan had always been the rock to his brother's rolling stone, especially when Ethan was in the Navy and off fighting in the Middle East. He'd felt alone in running the ranch those years, and he still felt alone in the battle —even though everyone kept telling him he was not.

He needed a rock, and he had to let his brothers shoulder some of the responsibility. Letting go was a difficult thing for him to do, though.

Evan was a loner. He might have to face it eventually, that he needed help.

The sound of paper slapping against the oak pedestal table jerked him out of his musing. "We probably need to open that and read it."

Evan's gaze lingered on his brother for a couple of seconds, then he glanced at the envelope. "What's it about?"

Ethan leaned back against the counter and sipped his coffee. "Not sure. Brandley brought it up from the mailbox last night."

Brandley had worked late the day before in Rapid City, having taken a side job to help see the ranch through. She had assumed the responsibility of buying groceries not long after she and Ethan married, saying it was her contribution to the family. An accountant, she occasionally took temporary jobs, besides running the books for Sweet Grass.

"It's from the bank."

Evan noticed the bank's logo in the corner and his gut twisted. "Shit." He stood motionless at the table, unsure whether to open the damn thing. He looked at his brother. "Does she have any idea what this could be?"

Ethan pushed away from the counter and took a couple of steps toward Evan. "She has an idea, but we need to read it."

Part of him wanted to hurl it away unopened. Keep pretending things weren't falling apart. But he snatched it up and slit it open with his pocketknife instead. He scanned the page.

"Damn it all to hell." Evan growled, crumpling the letter in his fist. He thought of his grandfather breaking the land generations earlier, his father instrumental in every building raised on the land, every animal fed and grown there, with MacKay sweat.

Evan's stubborn pride flared hot. Like hell he'd hand over their legacy without a fight. There had to be something he could do, some way to buy more time. Anything but throw in the towel.

He'd thought all the issues resolved. "We need to talk to Brandley. See where we went wrong." He passed the crumpled letter to his brother.

Ethan took longer to read it than Evan had. "It just says they want a meeting. No big deal. Let's not get worked up over it."

"Right."

"Who is this J. Chase? We've never dealt with a loan officer with that name before."

Stepping closer, Evan peered down at the letter. "No clue. If there is a new bastard at the bank who thinks he's going to rip in here and rob us of our ranch, our livelihood, call in the loans, well then—"

"Whoa," Ethan interrupted, setting the wrinkled letter on the counter. "Slow the hell down here. No one said anything about calling in any loans. You need to get a grip."

Raking a hand through his short hair, Evan shook his head. "I've been worked up since I saw that envelope."

"Hate to tell you, but you've been worked up over this for months. It's wearing on you."

Evan blew out a sharp breath. "Well, yeah, this kind of shit does that."

"We'll figure something out. The bank is only asking for a meeting. That doesn't mean anything other than this new guy is reviewing accounts."

Evan cut him off harshly. "Not sure about that." He paced, frustration boiling over. "I will not lose this place, you understand me? I won't."

"*We* won't." Ethan stayed calm. "And we will come up with a plan. You're not in this alone."

Evan paced and whirled back. "We had a plan. What the hell happened?"

"I know exactly what happened." Both brothers turned as Brandley pushed into the room. "The plan was solid, Evan. It was a good plan."

"You heard all that?"

She stared. "Everyone in the house heard you, Evan. You woke up the baby."

"Hell. I'm sorry." He lowered his voice. "Then what went wrong?"

With a sigh, Brandley continued. "We all know how Aaron and Aiden have struggled with the rodeo stock business. It just didn't take off like they expected. We lost money there."

Evan stared at Ethan. "You knew this?"

His brother eased out a slow breath. "Only because I sleep with the accountant."

"Dammit." Evan turned away. "Where are our little brothers? They have some explaining to do." He turned back and pointed at Ethan. "And no more rodeo. One of them is going to break their damn back riding those bulls and broncs. And then where would we be? One hand short?"

Ethan stared at him, that long, cool Navy SEAL stare that Evan never really knew, for sure, what it meant.

"You don't mean that," Ethan said. "It's time to calm down. I'll talk to the boys."

Brandley pulled down another coffee mug and lifted the carafe from the coffeemaker. "I can meet with the bank. I'll take that off your hands." She glanced down at the letter.

"No. I'll go," Evan said.

Ethan took another step. "No. We go together, and we face the fact that we can't handle this situation on our own. We may need help from somewhere."

Evan bristled. Asking for help stuck in his craw almost as much as bending a knee to the bank. But the steely look in Ethan's eyes held no argument. "We're not telling Mom. Not yet. Because you know what she will say."

"I do." Ethan stared. "Luckily, she's in Montana with Sarah and the new baby."

To be honest, Evan was glad his mother wasn't under foot and was off visiting their little sister. Maybe she'd stay in Montana for a while. "Right. I'm sure she's happy cuddling that new grandbaby."

Brandley snorted. "And cuddling her new husband."

"Yeah, well, there is that." It wasn't that Evan didn't like Noah Parker, he did. And the older cowboy was good for their mother. It was just hard to see her with anyone but their dad, even after he'd been gone a few years.

"Noah's a good man," Ethan said. "We don't have to worry about Mom, or Sarah, for that matter. They are both pretty much settled in Montana now."

"Let's just see what this loan officer has to say."

"I think this letter is pretty clear," Brandley interjected.

"They mean business. And while I know you two want to handle this on your own, remember that this ranch and everything on it is owned by your mother. You're going to have to bring Connie into this discussion sooner rather than later."

Much as it galled him, they were out of options. Brandley was right.

If it came to swallowing his pride or losing the ranch, the choice was obvious. "Alright. We will tell Mom after this meeting. Let's meet with this Chase guy and see what's what, but I'm damn well not giving up without a fight."

Ethan clasped his shoulder. "Expect nothing less from us all, brother."

* * *

The next morning, Evan was up before dawn. Nothing unusual. He headed out to the barn, the familiar smells of hay and horses bringing small comfort. Mornings were his favorite part of the day—his routine grounded him.

As he began his chores, checking each stall, feeding and watering the horses, his thoughts returned to the bank letter. He tried to push it from his mind, focusing instead on the simple rhythms of his work.

When he led the horses out to pasture, they trotted freely through the tall grass gleaming with dew. The sunrise painted a golden glow over the hills in hues of pink and orange while long shadows stretched across the land. Evan paused, watching as sunlight touched everything around him. The ranch was his life's work—every tree, shrub, and blade of grass felt like an old friend.

Throughout the day, they mended fences, inspected equipment. While he worked to keep his outward demeanor calm and focused, a deep worry settled inside him like a stone. He didn't say anything because words weren't what made things better.

Their actions were what would save this ranch.

When evening came, Evan sat on the porch, dusk gathering around him like a blanket. Another day's work. Just how they'd built this ranch one day after another of physical effort. He gazed out over the land and remembered all his grandfather and father had built there, all that they had built together, year after year of sweat and heartache.

He'd give anything to sit on the porch with his dad again, one last time, and talk over the day. He missed Hap MacKay like nothing he'd ever before experienced.

With a heavy sigh, he took off his hat and ran both hands over his head. "I don't know what we're going to do, Dad," he mumbled. "But I know one thing for certain. Whatever happens next, we'll meet it head-on, just like you tackled every challenge you ever met."

Chapter Two

J essica Chase strode through the glass doors into the marble-floored lobby of Cattlemens Bank & Trust in Rapid City, her new black patent-leather Jimmy Choo stilettos clicking with each self-assured step. She paused, taking in the hushed activity of tellers and patrons. In her first month as a newly hired loan manager, she reminded herself that this was the time to make a favorable impression.

Walking briskly to the elevators, she stood tall, wearing a crisp gray suit that complemented her long, dark hair. As she waited for the elevator, she tucked a stray strand over her ear, watched the numbers fall, and smiled with confidence.

I am going to do good things here.

The new job was her chance to prove herself on somewhat familiar turf. She'd been successful in New York City, and then in Cleveland. Now, a stone's throw away from where she'd grown up, she planned to be just as successful in Rapid City, South Dakota.

The elevator arrived with a soft chime and Jessica stepped inside, her posture straight and poised. As the floors ticked by, she mentally prepared for the meeting with the senior manager who had hired her. She would show him she understood what it took to be successful at Cattlemens—and that she could deliver.

The doors slid open. Jessica headed down the hallway, her gait oozing with confidence. Her rural roots would not hold her back. She'd done well as a city girl. Time to prove her worth back on home turf, in rural America, doing something she'd always wanted to do—help the ranchers.

Meeting with Lance Nelson was part of her orientation, and she was eager to get the meeting started.

Stepping into his outer office, she smiled at Jill McCandless, his administrative assistant, who nodded back while talking on the phone. She'd met Jill a couple of weeks earlier. "I'm here for my onboarding with Mr. Nelson," she whispered.

Jill put the caller on hold and pointed to the door on her right. "He's expecting you. Just give it a quick knock before you enter, will you? I need to finish this call."

"Of course."

Pausing outside the senior manager's door, Jessica drew in a breath, knocked, and placed a hand on the doorknob.

"Come in."

She entered the office, immediately noting its dark wood furnishings and massive mahogany desk. Behind it sat Mr. Nelson, a stern-looking older man in a tailored suit.

"Ah, Ms. Chase. Please have a seat." He didn't look up from the file on his desk. She guessed he assumed it was her because of the appointment time.

Jessica sat in one of the leather chairs facing him, her back straight and hands folded neatly over the leather portfolio on her lap. She focused intently on Mr. Nelson, determined to show her readiness and take copious notes if necessary.

After a moment, he closed the file and peered over his glasses. "Welcome to Cattlemens, Miss Chase. I think you'll find we have high standards here."

"Yes sir. I'm prepared to do whatever it takes to meet those standards."

"Good. You came highly recommended, and that increases my expectations. Plus, I understand you've been assigned one of our most high-profile accounts—Sweet Grass Ranch."

Jessica's eyes widened slightly. The ranch was one of the area's largest and oldest family operations. Its accounts were complex, to be certain. "Yes, sir. I started my review of the portfolio earlier in the week and have already taken some action."

"Excellent. I trust, then, you are up to speed."

"I am getting there. Yes."

Mr. Nelson continued. "The fate of Sweet Grass affects this entire community. I need someone who can handle it properly." He snorted softly and grinned to himself as he stared back down at his paperwork.

"Of course. I'll do my best, sir."

Properly? And just what does that mean? She'd been around the block enough to know that sometimes businesses had a certain lingo with underlying meanings. She sure hoped *properly* meant exactly how it sounded.

Jessica was a by-the-book girl, so she certainly hoped he wasn't implying that she should do anything different. Numbers don't lie, and she always called them as she saw them. As they were. And that's what she planned to continue doing.

"That's why we hired you."

"Absolutely, sir. I'll account for every detail and explore all options to keep the ranch accounts solvent." *I will not fail.*

"Very well." He stood and gave her a quick once-over. "If you have questions, speak with Jill. She's been here for some time."

My cue to leave. That was quick.

She stood, too, and pushed out her hand. "I appreciate the opportunity."

He gave her hand a brief glance, then finally shook it. Perhaps she should have waited for him to offer his hand first, immediately reminded that she wasn't back east. It was a man's world there in the west.

I really do have some things to prove here. And learn.

"Thank you, Mr. Nelson." With a nod, she turned and left, her mind racing ahead to the task at hand. Time to show them what she could do.

* * *

Jessica walked briskly down the hallway to her new office. As she entered the small, tidy space, she sat behind her desk and took a deep breath. She wasn't the kind to go overboard personalizing things—largely because she wanted to appear rather impersonal to her clients—but also because she liked to spend time in a new place before deciding how to make it hers.

She glanced at the lone picture on her desk. Someone took the photo a long time ago—she may have been eight or nine years old—but she couldn't remember who. It was at her grandparents' ranch. The barn and corral with horses were in the background. Her parents and grandparents were in the forefront, smiling at the camera. She stood in front of her dad, who had his hands on her shoulders. Her mother smiled at him from the side.

She studied the little girl in the photo. The picture was far from flattering, with her wayward hair and freckled nose and worn-out dirty jeans, but she had really cheesed it up for the camera. She was happy then. Everyone she loved was there, and her father, with his protective hands on her shoulders, had made her feel so safe.

Funny how things could take a turn so quickly.

She glanced at the folder on her desk.

This is it. The Sweet Grass Ranch account would make or break her career.

She knew when a ranch failed, that other ranchers in the area got nervous. The bank would get anxious, too. Of course, the Sweet Grass Ranch issues came about over time and circumstance—but ranchers know situations can happen to any ranch. Which ranch might be next? They all work hard to stay afloat from year to year, and there were way too many factors that could make a ranch go down.

She knew that first-hand. While she had to prove herself to the bank, she also wanted to help the ranchers keep their lifestyle and preserve their livelihood for generations to come.

An enormous task, but she was ready for it.

Logging into her computer, she pulled up the Sweet Grass file, reviewing the cattle ranch's history. Established in the early 1900s, it had been family-owned for generations. But in recent years, there were troubling signs, such as declines in profits and missed loan payments.

Making notes on a legal pad, she analyzed cash flow, debt ratios, and collateral. Her career in commercial lending had prepared her well for meticulous scrutiny.

A knock at the door a few hours later brought a cart loaded with heavy binders—the physical files on decades of loans she had requested. Jessica signed for the documents, then stacked them on her desk. She opened the top one to scan its contents.

She needed an intimate understanding of the financial ebbs and flows of the ranch in order to identify the root causes of their struggles. Only then could she develop an effective strategy to put them back on solid footing.

In the beginning, things looked stable. Steady profits, manageable debt, reserves set aside for hard times. Father and son, Lucas and Hap MacKay, conservatively ran the operation initially—that would be the grandfather and father of the brothers who now ran the ranch.

But after Lucas MacKay died, Hap gained control, and over time, cracks appeared in the foundation. Small loans were not repaid on time; supplies were charged against credit that wasn't there. Signs of cash flow issues emerged.

Jessica had to wonder if Hap MacKay had an unhealthy connection with the bank that allowed such behavior.

At the time of Hap's death, problems escalated. Hap's wife, Connie, inherited the ranch when he died, but the two older sons had since taken over its management. They, too, made some questionable decisions. More debt, new equipment leased, repairs deferred. Revenue declined as costs rose.

Two years earlier, they'd worked with the bank to create a five-year recovery plan, which they were currently executing. To a degree.

There were still issues. The ranch was struggling.

Jessica could see the path that led to the brink of insolvency. Poor financial management, risky purchases, emotional decisions, lack of experience. She ached for the family even as her analytical mind identified the missteps.

She was certain she could fix them, especially if the family didn't mind getting creative.

Perhaps they could establish an on-site farmer's market for their organic beef? Or transition part of their land to a more profitable crop? She scribbled ideas, determined to find an answer.

The clock edged toward evening as Jessica studied spreadsheets lit by the amber glow of her desk lamp. The MacKay family's livelihood depended on her ability to resolve their crisis. She had to succeed.

With a tired sigh, she organized her notes and files into neat piles. As she clicked off the lamp, her gaze lingered on the photos of rolling hills and grazing cattle that decorated her office —standard office issue, she imagined. Nevertheless, they reminded her of Wyoming and rekindled her resolve.

There was still hope for Sweet Grass Ranch, if the MacKays were ready to accept hard truths. Jessica knew she could guide them if they would let her. In some ways, she'd been there herself. Or rather, her family had. She would need to draw on that experience more than ever.

* * *

Before noon the next day, Jessica set the files aside, leaned back in her chair, removed her glasses, and rubbed her gritty eyes. She'd worked too long into the night, and from way too early that morning. Her eyes were paying the price, but the story of Sweet Grass Ranch was becoming clear. She only needed to fill in some missing pieces.

Picking up the phone, she dialed the number for the MacKay ranch. A man answered on the third ring.

"Evan MacKay, here."

One of the brothers. Good.

"Mr. MacKay, I'm calling from Cattlemens Bank. I'm reviewing your ranch's file."

"Alright." Evan MacKay sounded wary, but polite as he responded. "We got a letter."

"Yes. That went out earlier this week."

"Are you calling to schedule a meeting, as the letter suggested? We would like to discuss. My brother and I, and our accountant."

Jessica drummed her fingers on the desk. "I think that would be best. I have questions." She glanced at her calendar. "Could you meet Monday morning at ten?"

A brief silence met her from the other end.

"We will be there Monday morning."

"I'll get you in the schedule. Thank you."

"Of course."

"Mr. MacKay, I know this is difficult. Cattlemens just wants to help Sweet Grass Ranch get back on solid footing."

Evan MacKay hung up without another word.

Jessica gazed out the window. She understood their deep connection to the land and way of life. Losing the ranch would be devastating. Her job was to make sure that didn't happen—while at the same time, protecting the bank's investment.

Chapter Three

Evan moved over the threshold and into the small wood-paneled conference room, his worn cowboy boots scuffing against the polished hardwood floor. Ethan and Brandley followed a step behind him. As soon as he entered the room, the woman sitting at the table, focused on a stack of paperwork, drew his attention. Her dark hair, pulled back in a low, sleek ponytail, trailed down her back. Diamond stud earrings glinted as she looked up.

He stepped forward. "I'm Evan MacKay. We're here to meet with Mr. Chase," he said, clearing his throat.

The woman smiled. "Nice to meet you. I'm Jessica Chase."

Evan felt his eyes go wide and big, his assumptions thoroughly overturned. *She is J. Chase? I'll be damned.*

She rose. "Everyone, please take a seat." She gestured to the leather chairs across the table from her and looked directly at Evan. "We spoke on the phone."

Evan sank into the leather seat, darting an uncertain glance at Ethan and Brandley as they settled into chairs beside him.

"Right. I just... I assumed... Hell." Evan's voice trailed off as Jessica pinned him with a pointed look.

"You assumed I was an administrative assistant sitting here, and also when I called you the other day to set up an appointment, and that J. Chase was a man," she finished, one perfectly shaped eyebrow raised.

Brandley stifled a giggle.

Heat crept up his neck. Evan hated to admit she was right. He definitely hadn't expected a polished and sophisticated woman. Not that a woman couldn't grasp or understand the ins and outs of running a ranch—his mother would tan his hide, even at his age, if he admitted that.

But what did this Jessica Chase know about the backbreaking work of ranching? The heartache of losing cattle to harsh winters, the legacy of a family ranch lifestyle? All their loan officers in the past had been men, and most of them ranchers. The woman looked like she'd just stepped out of a New York City taxicab.

Ethan shot him a warning look, as if he could read his mind.

Brandley scooted to the edge of her seat and leaned forward. "Ms. Chase, I'm Brandley MacKay, the ranch accountant, and Ethan's wife." She nodded toward her husband. "We appreciate your time meeting with us, and I'm happy to answer any questions you might have."

Ethan angled her way, too. "As you know, the ranch has hit some hard times the past few years, but we're committed to finding a solution."

Ms. Jessica Chase shuffled through the paperwork on her desk and Evan watched intently.

"Yes, of course." She arranged a few more things, then looked up, briefly making eye contact with each of them. "Why don't you walk me through the current financial situation from your perspectives, and then we can discuss how I am seeing things."

Evan shifted in his seat, his earlier assumptions warring with a grudging admiration for the woman's directness.

She exuded an air of competence, her gaze sharp and assessing. Perhaps she knew a thing or two about ranching and land management, he couldn't say. Either way, Evan realized they would have to work together. He straightened in his seat and figured he could give her a fair chance. There was too much at stake not to.

"Now, who wants to start?" she began. "Tell me the story of Sweet Grass Ranch."

* * *

Evan let Ethan and Brandley lead the conversation. He supposed they could tell he was a bit on edge—which he was—and thought it best they jump in first. So be it. Ms. Jessica Chase appeared to listen carefully as Ethan summarized the ranch history, and Brandley reviewed the ranch's financial woes.

Evan kept quiet.

"I have a few questions," she said. "More about recent events, rather than history."

Ethan shifted closer. "We're happy to answer them, if we can."

Brandley agreed.

Jessica gave them a quick nod. "Alright. Let's start with the herd. Your numbers declined about twenty percent over the last two years. Can you tell me more about that?"

Ethan sighed. "We've had a string of bad luck. Lost some cattle to illness and sold off others to cover costs. Prices are high right now. Haven't been able to restock."

Jessica jotted notes as Ethan spoke.

"We tried another tactic," Brandley interjected. "We launched a rodeo stock business two years ago because the younger boys, Aaron and Aiden, are very connected to rodeo. Our thinking was leasing stock to events. This was a plan approved by the previous loan officer. Turned out with this inflation, the expenses for gas and hauling and hotels and food were more than we expected. We lost money."

Jessica studied Brandley. "Are you closing that business?"

"I think we should," Brandley offered. "The boys will resist, though."

The loan officer huffed out a breath. "You should sunset that business. I've reviewed those financials and see no successful path forward. The business cost more money than it brought in. Don't allow the boys to make an emotional decision that could lead to losing the ranch since they are not involved in the finances. My advice would be to dissolve what you have there, liquidate any assets you can, pay off debt, and move on."

Brandley sighed and nodded. "I'll get on that. We have stock and equipment we can sell."

"Good. The bank sees that as a favorable step forward."

Her next question centered on equipment. "I noticed a lot of repair bills for tractors, balers, parts, and such. Have you considered buying new, rather than repairing? I know ranch implements are expensive, but at some point, you can't keep fixing the older models, which are nearly obsolete and won't efficiently do the job. New equipment could act as collateral if needed."

Ethan explained they kept repairing the older models instead of upgrading because of the costs. They didn't want to borrow more from the bank.

"I understand these are tough decisions," she said. Turning to Evan, she added, "And what's your take on all this, Mr. MacKay?"

Evan bristled at her tone, sitting up a little straighter. "My take? My take is that the bank's been ready to foreclose for months now. Forgive me if I'm skeptical that you want to help."

Jessica's eyes flashed. She waited a moment before responding. "I understand, Mr. MacKay. You're hesitant. I want you to know I am very serious about my job. I am committed to finding the best solution for everyone."

"Yeah. I'm sure." Evan glanced up at the framed degrees on her wall. "Impressive."

"Excuse me?"

He continued to peruse the documents. "An MBA from NYU. Undergraduate work from Boston College." He pulled his gaze away. "I'm sure you learned a helluva lot about cows and horses and baling twine in those courses back east, ma'am."

Jessica eyed him. "You are making some bold assumptions."

"You know nothing about cattle ranching." For some odd reason, Evan enjoyed poking at the spunk in this woman.

"I know a lot about how to run a business."

"That right? And how many seasons have you spent busting your back on a ranch, Ms. Chase?" Evan shot back, leaning forward. "How many calves have you pulled in below-zero temperatures? Do you know what it takes to keep a ranch running in the dead of winter?"

Jessica's expression remained impassive. "I'm here to discuss finances, not ranching itself. My role is to assess the numbers and viability of the business."

Evan snorted cynically. "Yeah, you crunch your numbers. But we're the ones with mud on our boots, blood and sweat in the soil. This land's been in my family for generations. Don't pretend you know anything about that kind of sacrifice."

Ethan touched his arm. "Evan...."

Jessica's eyes flickered again, but her voice remained steady. Her chest rose with a deep breath, and she exhaled slowly between pursed lips. Red lips. He was getting under her skin, he knew, and suddenly, he didn't care.

Or was she getting under his?

"I understand this is an emotional issue, Mr. MacKay. But if we're to find a solution, and save your ranch, we'll need to have an open exchange of information—and speak cordially and candidly."

"I think I was fairly candid."

"That you were. Let me emphasize cordially, then."

Evan fumed but said nothing. The woman had a point, as much as he hated to admit it. If they were going to fix all this, they'd have to find some common ground.

He glanced off quickly, then caught her eye again. "Fine."

"Trust me," she said, staring. "You need me on your side."

Her gaze held his for several heartbeats, and suddenly Evan was at a loss for words.

She dismissed him, turning to Brandley. "Let's you and I set an appointment for next week to discuss this past year, financially speaking. I think we can come to some short-term decisions. I have a few ideas."

Glancing his way, and then to Ethan, Brandley agreed. "I'm all for ideas at this point."

"Great." Jessica opened a file. "We can schedule a meeting on your way out. But before you go, I have a quick question. Look here, in early January...."

Evan sat back in his chair, trying to rein in his frustration. As much as this female banker grated on him, he had to remind himself that she held the keys to securing financing for the ranch.

Ethan slid him a sneer—a warning look that he'd disapproved of his grumpy behavior—but said nothing. Evan predicted a lively discussion in the truck heading home.

He studied Jessica Chase more closely as she shuffled

through documents. Her ponytail was slung over her shoulder now, her dark hair a stark contrast to her crisp white blouse, which was unbuttoned three buttons down—not that he was counting. Or noticing. Not exactly rancher's attire. Of course, she was a banker, not a rancher. Still, he noted the subtle strength in her slender frame and the quick intelligence behind her eyes.

As she launched into figures and projections, Evan felt his attention drifting to the curve of her jawbone and the lilt of her voice. *Get it together,* he scolded himself. *You need to focus on the numbers, not get distracted by her pretty face.*

But despite his misgivings, he couldn't deny a grudging admiration for this woman who was holding her own against his gruff demeanor.

Evan shifted in his seat, suddenly feeling warm. The banker was trouble. The kind of trouble it would be easy to fall into if he wasn't careful. With effort, he tuned back into the conversation, focusing on Brandley and Ethan, determined to keep the relationship strictly business.

* * *

Jessica kept her gaze steady on the documents in front of her. Years of experience enabled her to exude a calm confidence, even as her pulse quickened under his intense scrutiny. Evan MacKay apparently couldn't keep his eyes off her.

Interesting.

She had expected resistance, but the animosity radiating off him was unmistakable. Still, she was determined to push through and do her job. Growing up on a ranch had taught her grit. Hell, life had taught her grit. She would prove to Evan that she knew the business and was good at her job.

Taking a deep breath, she refocused. Though sympathetic

to the MacKays' struggles, she knew a sentimental approach would not solve their problems.

"The bank is prepared to restructure your operating loan," she said to all three of them, her gaze landing on Evan. "Please realize this is a temporary solution. Restructuring will help in the short term, but the long game must sustainably grow your income and pay off your debts. We are not there yet."

Evan's eyes flashed. Hazel, she thought. Not green, not brown. In between. She glanced from one dark-haired brother to the other, sitting there with their hats on their laps. Identical twins, and quite handsome ones, too—fit from working the ranches and oozing no-nonsense demeanors.

"Just keeping the wolves at bay for the night. Right?" Evan said.

"What?"

He leaned closer. "Your tactic here—just keeping the wolves at bay?"

Dammit. Had she gotten distracted? "Oh, yes. Something like that."

"How long is the short term?" Brandley asked.

She returned her attention to the accountant, glad to focus anywhere but on the grumpy cowboy sitting across from her. "At six months, we will evaluate. If things go well, we will extend. If not, we'll call in the loans."

Evan leaned in. "On what terms?"

"Pay in full within sixty days or face foreclosure."

Evan stood. "That's not enough time to affect any sort of change. Winter is coming."

Jessica stood too, facing him. "I understand. We'll need to see some changes in how you manage your herds and winter feed. In the meantime, we'll also need an inventory of equipment and other assets and their worth—what can be fixed, what can be sold, and so on. Plus, dissolving the rodeo stock business, as discussed. I hope you will agree, because frankly, you don't have much choice."

Evan jerked. "Now, just a minute. No banker's going to tell me how to run my ranch."

Jessica held up a hand. "Mr. MacKay, I know you want what's best for your family. I do too. If we don't make some adjustments, you risk losing it all. Agreeing to this is a first step to an acceptable solution for both parties—your family and the bank."

Evan stared, the tension between them crackling. Then he let out a long breath, his shoulders slumping slightly. "Alright then. Fine."

Jessica nodded, feeling a bit of relief. She could hold her own in confrontation, but that didn't mean she liked it. This wouldn't be easy, but it was a start. She could be patient with Evan MacKay. She'd grown up with stubborn cowboys and had elbowed her way through the male-dominated financial world. Despite their differences, she recognized in Evan the same deep love of the land and way of life she'd grown up with. That understanding might be the thing to help them find common ground.

She glanced from Brandley to Ethan, and then back to Evan. "I'd like a tour of the ranch. Are you up for that?"

Evan spoke up. "Not a problem."

"Great. I'll see you tomorrow morning at eight o'clock. That work?" Jessica closed her leather folder.

Evan smiled. "Why so late?"

Jessica cocked her head, gave him a stare, and smiled. "Make it seven."

"I'll be on my second pot of coffee by then."

"Perfect. Make mine black."

Chapter Four

van stood at the edge of the wide porch, boots scuffing against the weathered boards as he scanned the long dirt road leading up to the ranch house. The second pot of coffee was brewing in the kitchen, and the mug full he had in his hand was hot. He took a sip and hoped Jessica Chase indeed liked hers strong.

He shifted his weight from one foot to the other, fingers drumming an impatient rhythm on the porch railing. Where was she? *Ms. High and Mighty* from back east, coming to tell him how to run the ranch that he and his family had successfully run for generations. His jaw clenched at the thought.

But deep inside, he knew that the word successfully was a bit misplaced, and that feeling ate at his gut.

This wasn't on his shoulders alone—but that sense of being alone was difficult to shake. Ethan had been away for years, serving his country. He returned home injured and battered, unable to do physical work for quite some time. Dylan had always worked off the ranch and while he helped as much as he could, his priority was law enforcement. Sarah had a music career that took her off the ranch at eighteen, and was now married with a baby, and making her life in Montana. And the younger twins? All they wanted to do was play—rodeo.

When his father died, the responsibility fell on his shoulders. So perhaps he was the one at fault, unable to pull up the bootstraps and get it done.

So yeah. That was his battle to fight.

In the distance, the rolling hills stretched as far as he could see, miles of endless prairie and scrub grass. Overhead, the sky blazed cobalt, cloudless and infinite. This land was in his blood, deep as bone. And no outsider was going to tell him how to manage it. He'd given his whole life to the ranch, just as his father and grandfather had before him.

A plume of dirt swirled up from the road as a newer model SUV came into view, glinting in the sun as it rumbled up the lane. His shoulders tensed, fingers curling around the mug.

The black Tahoe pulled up in front of the house, its polished rims and spotless exterior jarringly out of place against the ranch setting. Dust billowed around, peppering the windshield and windows as it came to a stop, and the engine was cut off.

The driver's side door swung open and out stepped Ms. Jessica Chase. She wore a black business suit—a skirt this time rather than pants—with a baby blue shirt underneath. Evan normally didn't notice such things, but the V-neck of her shirt plunged a mite lower than he'd seen on most professional women—not that he was in the habit of ogling professional women. He wasn't. Her black heels looked a little deadly. Today, her equally dark hair was swept up in a neat twist.

He decided he'd probably like her hair down better. Flowing free.

But who was he to have an opinion?

No one, that was for sure. Not where her hair was concerned.

Or her plunging neckline.

Reaching for her briefcase from inside the SUV, her skirt rode up a little from behind, showing quite a bit of leg. Ethan turned away, taking a sip of coffee, and pacing off to the left, looking toward the barn.

She slammed the vehicle door, and he turned back around at the sound.

Jessica approached, surveying her surroundings as she slowly walked toward Evan and met him on the top porch step.

He looked her up and down. Clearly, she wasn't the type to get her hands dirty. The woman didn't know the first thing about the realities of the ranch. All she cared about was numbers on a page.

"Ms. Chase," he said gruffly, giving a curt nod.

"Mr. MacKay," she replied smoothly, extending her hand. He stared at it briefly, then shook it. He almost wanted to make an excuse for his calloused palm against her soft palm—then thought the hell with it. Ranchers have callouses.

"I'm surprised you drive an SUV," he said, gesturing to her vehicle. "I figured you for more of a sports car type."

She raised an eyebrow. "Going off stereotypes, are we?" Her tone was clipped, businesslike. "I grew up in Wyoming. I know a thing or two about back roads."

Evan crossed his arms, looking her up and down skeptically. "From Wyoming to Boston, huh?"

"And back again." She jerked a grin. "With a couple of other cities in between."

Jessica met his gaze steadily. Perhaps expecting his skepticism? Was it that obvious he thought she didn't belong there?

"I know you have doubts," she began. "You don't think I understand what it takes to run a ranch this size. But I'm here to help, not criticize."

She paused, as if carefully choosing her next words. "My

job is to ensure the long-term viability of this operation. Your ranch. That requires a detached assessment of the financials and the assets—where money is coming in, where it's going out, and what is of value. I won't pretend to know the intricate details of cattle ranching."

Evan snorted. "Intricate details? Lady, you don't know the first thing about it. Ranching is more than numbers in a spreadsheet. It's early mornings and late nights. Sunup to sundown."

"I understand that, Mr. MacKay, although spreadsheets can be your friend if you will let them. As long as we can execute the plan discussed yesterday, things will be fine. I would like to further lay out for you today, then—"

"That's the problem!" He interrupted, jabbing a forefinger in the air, a fire suddenly in his gut. "We've scraped by on hard work and grit for three generations. I won't have some out-of-town banker telling us how to live our lives or run our ranch."

Jessica arched a brow at his outburst, meeting his gaze without so much of a flinch. She responded, her tone soft. "Evan, I'm not here to fight you. My goal is the same as yours, to ensure Sweet Grass Ranch survives. Let's work on that. Together."

Evan. Not Mr. MacKay.

He was a bit taken aback by the sound of his name coming from her lips, but perhaps more so by her sincerity. He stood silently. Conflicting emotions played across his chest. "Alright. Let's do that tour. See if you can keep up."

Jessica smiled. "Oh, I intend to."

* * *

Steadying herself with a deep inhale, Jessica stepped around Evan and moved across the sweeping porch, gazing out over the endless hills. This land represented everything Evan held dear.

She knew that, understood that. Blood, sweat and sacrifice. She also knew he saw her as an outsider, maybe even an enemy.

She couldn't reveal her truth, though. Not yet. That she, too, had grown up on a ranch much like Sweet Grass. Had risen before dawn to help with chores, watched in awe as new calves entered the world, cried when drought took its toll.

No, she needed to prove herself first, not only to Evan but all the MacKays. She needed him to see her as more than just a banker in high heels.

Turning, she met his skeptical gaze. "Where do we start?"

He swept an arm toward the front door. "The ranch office is right inside."

"Excellent."

They moved into the sprawling log cabin, down the hall and to the left, to the office.

Jessica sat her papers on the desk, flipped open the top folder and pulled out a spreadsheet, laying it on top of a pile of bills. She peripherally noted the large cherry desk, leather furnishings, and a few hunting trophies mounted on the walls.

She pointed to the printed spreadsheet. "As you can see here, reducing your herd size by ten percent will significantly cut down on your operating expenses," she began.

Evan leaned over the desk, scanning the numbers with a furrowed brow. His worn boots and faded jeans nudged her pumps, and a warmth traveled up her leg that she tried to ignore.

"No way we're culling that many cattle. We're already low in numbers."

Jessica kept her tone even. "I understand, but you simply can't sustain. The market's down and your margins are razor thin as it is."

"We'll make it work. We always have."

"Selling ten percent will also supply cash in hand. Cash you need to repair that fence on the south side of the barn." She stood tall and looked directly into his eyes.

Evan stared back. "Who told you about the fence?"

"No one. I noticed the leaning fence posts on my drive back here."

Evan looked a little befuddled. "Suddenly everyone's an expert."

Jessica bit back a retort, reminding herself that she needed to win over the stubborn cowboy. Time for a different tactic.

"I grew up on a ranch in Wyoming," she said conversationally. "My family went through some tough years, too. But with some adjustments, we survived." *For a few years, at least.* But she didn't want to tell him that right now. "This ranch will too, but you have some hard decisions ahead."

Evan looked surprised, then narrowed his eyes. "Why didn't you say something before?"

"About growing up on a ranch?"

"Yes."

She shrugged, avoiding his gaze. "Didn't seem relevant. The point is, I know what it takes to run a ranch. While I have spent a few years in the city, I'm not only some city slicker, as you assumed."

Evan rubbed his jaw. Perhaps his resistance was wavering?

Time to press her advantage.

"Why don't we go over the rest of this?" she suggested. "I'm sure we can find an approach that makes sense for Sweet Grass that won't be too painful."

Evan sighed, then gave a grudging nod. "Alright, let's take a look."

She bit back a smile. The hard part was over. Now to show this cranky cowboy she was there to help, not just crunch numbers. She returned their attention to the spreadsheet. "Here's where your costs shot up for feed and fuel. Since the herd is smaller, if we can renegotiate your land leases, that could offset some of it."

Evan rubbed his stubbled jaw as he studied the numbers. "Reckon you've got a point there," he conceded.

"And," she continued, "have you discussed selling the rodeo stock and dissolving that business with Aaron and Aiden?"

"Ethan is handling that with the boys."

"Great. That will help. If there is equipment—shoots, pens, trailers, tack that was used specifically for that business—sell that off too. Anything you don't need for running the cattle operation. You might try some of the rodeo buy, swap, and sell sites online. Have the boys do it."

Evan's head dipped in a nod. "Alright. Got that too."

Jessica smiled. "See? I know a thing or two about making things work."

Their eyes met, and Evan gave her a considering look. "Maybe you do at that."

Jessica felt an unexpected warmth in her chest at his words. She knew she didn't need this slightly pig-headed cowboy's approval, but somehow, she wanted it.

"How about we grab some coffee and keep talking?" Evan suggested. "I want to hear more of your ideas."

Is that a fresh note of respect I detect in your voice? "I have a better idea. How about we take that ranch tour now? When we get back, perhaps Brandley and Ethan can join us."

"That can be arranged. Might as well see how you handle getting your fancy shoes dirty."

Cute. He could be personable, after all. "Lead the way, cowboy."

Evan almost grinned, seemed to her.

As they strolled through the house, Jessica took in the warm, cozy atmosphere of the home—the rich wood tones balanced with soft leather. They exited the house through a side entrance and made their way toward the barns and outbuildings.

Evan explained more about the ranch's operations, who handled what, and the number of ranch hands who worked for them. A spark of anticipation sent a slight tremor through her. This unlikely partnership might work after all. Underneath that rugged exterior, the cowboy had more depth than she realized. And despite herself, she was looking forward to finding out more.

"Tell me. How'd a woman like you get into the banking business?"

Jessica hesitated. That question took her a little off guard.

Should she confess the entire story of her ranching roots? "I've always been good at numbers and money. I worked as a teller in college, and discovered I enjoyed banking, too. It was a natural fit. Also..." She gazed up into the hills behind the buildings. "I wanted to help ranchers like you. I know firsthand the challenges you face."

Evan cocked a brow. "Firsthand?"

"Yes." Jessica looked away, then at her watch. "Oh. I better check in with the office," she said, skirting his question. "Let them know I'm coming in a little later than normal." She wasn't ready to reveal herself just yet.

"Fine. Make your call and then meet me back here at the barn. We'll take the Jeep up into the hills to get a bird's-eye view of the place."

"Sounds great. Thanks."

Evan didn't press and simply stepped away. Jessica felt a conflicting pang of relief and regret. She wanted Evan to see her as more than a banker but opening that wound from her past was not something she was ready to share. Yet.

* * *

A few minutes later, Evan covertly observed Jessica from the driver's side of the Jeep as they toured the ranch, sneaking a glance at her now and then, and thoughtfully responding to her questions. Though initially skeptical, he couldn't help but admire her quick intelligence and thorough questions. Clearly, she had done her homework.

"This is beautiful country. I can see why your family works so hard to preserve it."

Surprised, Evan turned to face her. The late morning sun lit her features with a soft glow. For the first time, he noticed the flecks of gold in her eyes.

"My grandfather built this place from the ground up," he said after a moment. "He's touched every fence post, every board in that barn over there. It's not just land to us. It's his legacy."

Jessica nodded slowly. "I understand." She paused, a faraway look in her eyes. "I know what it's like to have roots sunk deep in a place."

Evan raised an eyebrow, intrigued by the peek into her past. Before he could ask more about her life, Jessica gave him a frank look and changed the subject.

"I won't pretend to know ranching like you do. You're right in some ways. I'm all about numbers. But I know the value of preserving something meaningful." She gestured back towards the ranch house. "Let me help you do that."

Evan studied her for a long moment. The breeze lifted strands of her dark hair from its sleekly coiled knot at the back of her head and swept them across her face. She brushed the strands out of her eyes before he could gather up the courage to do it for her.

Finally, he gave a single nod.

"Alright then," he said. "We've got ourselves a deal."

Chapter Five

Leaning on the handle of his shovel, Evan swiped a clinging row of sweat from his brow and surveyed the half-finished south pasture fence. While the weather was turning cooler, the late morning sun still beat hot against his back, as he and Ethan worked to finish the repairs before the colder weather set in.

"I know you didn't want to reduce the herd," Ethan said, pausing his work beside him, "but we wouldn't have been able to get this fence fixed otherwise."

Evan knew that statement was the truth. It had been a week since they'd culled the herd, sold most of the rodeo stock, and had created some cash flow. But while their financial situation was better temporarily, they were no way near out of the woods.

"We only have six months to get this right. This bank plan better work, or we're sunk." Evan watched the crew down the fence line, doing their part. Sometimes he looked at the men working for him, and his stomach turned. The ranch supported more families than his own. What would those men do without their jobs if he lost the ranch? "These patchwork repairs will hold for this winter and spring, but this entire fence has to be replaced before next fall. I bet some of these posts are over a hundred years old."

Ethan drove a post-hole digger into the hard earth with a grunt. "I know. I don't like it either, but we're out of options. Let's just get the work done and hope Jessica continues to come through. I really do think she is trying to keep the wolf from the door."

A cloud of dust billowed in the distance, signaling the approach of a vehicle. The brothers looked up as an older model pickup truck rambled up the ranch road. Evan squinted against the bright sunlight, trying to make out who it might be.

"Is that Mom?" Ethan asked, shielding his eyes with his hand. "Looks like Noah's truck."

"Could be," Evan replied cautiously, his gut tightening.

As the truck drew closer and parked, its occupants came into view.

"Oh, hell. It is Mom."

"I thought they were still visiting with Sarah and the baby."

Noah Parker and Connie MacKay had married a few weeks back. Prior to getting married, they'd divided their time between Sweet Grass Ranch and Noah's home at Rock Creek Ranch in Paradise Valley, Montana.

Noah stepped out of the truck from the driver's side, gave the boys a wave, then moved to help their mother on the passenger side. She rounded the truck, waving vigorously and shouting.

"Guess they're back."

Ethan put a hand on Evan's shoulder, a subtle restraint. "Let's see what's going on." He leaned a shovel against the fence post.

The brothers ambled toward the house and the waiting couple.

"I'll bet you dollars for donuts she's been talking with our sister."

Evan halted, looking at his brother. "Did you say anything to Sarah about the bank?"

"Brandley talks to her all the time. I'm sure the subject of the ranch came up. Should she not talk to her about it? She needs to be informed, just like the rest of us."

Evan forcefully exhaled. "But did Brandley tell Sarah not to tell Mom?"

"I haven't a clue. I'm just speculating."

Reluctantly, Evan nodded and forced his fists to uncurl as their mother approached. Without a word, she put her arms around her two tall cowboy sons and hugged them best she could. They reciprocated, and she stepped back.

"You two need to stop growing."

Ethan chuckled. "Mom, we stopped growing fifteen years ago. We're thirty-six years old."

She waved that statement away. "I'm glad to see you." Then she reached for Noah and took his hand. "We are glad to see you."

Evan tipped his hat. "Noah."

Ethan reached out a hand. "Sir."

Noah laughed and shook it. "Now stop that sir shit. I'm just Noah. Good to see you both."

Connie beamed, looking from her sons to her new husband.

"So, how was the Cabo honeymoon?"

"Beautiful. But we're glad to be home."

Evan wondered if there was more to that statement. "Home? Have you two decided where you are going to live? Here or in Montana?"

"Well...." Noah began.

Connie cut him off, snatching out to grasp both her son's hands. "That's what we want to talk to you both about. The rest of the family, too." She spoke warmly, but there was an underlying tension in her words. "We have some news."

Evan exchanged a wary glance with Ethan. "Mom? What's going on?"

Connie hesitated, her eyes flicking between her sons. She took a deep breath. "We... Noah and I... Well, we think we have a way to help with the ranch problems."

Her words hung heavy in the air. Evan's heart raced as he tried to process the information, his mind already leaping to conclusions about the future of Sweet Grass Ranch. Beside him, Ethan remained silent, his face betraying nothing.

"Help? What do you mean?"

"We'll explain everything," Connie said gently, her eyes filled with a mixture of hope and trepidation. "Please, just trust me. I've already talked with Sarah. Now, when can we get everyone together?"

Ethan tossed Evan a look. "Well, the boys are in Denver, their last rodeo before coming back to work full time again. Dylan is in training in Billings. So, it might be another week before—"

"That's right. I forgot about Dylan. I saw him a few days ago." Connie cut him off. "Never mind. Let's talk tonight at dinner. What I have to say won't wait until everyone gets back home. The two of you are officially the managers of this ranch, so you need to know what I am thinking." She dropped her son's hands, smiled at Noah, and tucked her right hand into his left elbow. "We're heading up to the cabin. I'll fix dinner tonight. Pretty sure there are steaks in the freezer. We'll pull out the grill this afternoon and get it cleaned up. See you both at seven."

And with that, Connie and Noah headed back to the truck.

Evan eased out a sigh through his teeth. "Shit."

"Yeah."

"Best get that fence done."

"Yeah."

"What the hell does she have up her sleeve?" Evan watched them head up the hill, dust flying behind the pickup.

Ethan shook his head. "No clue."

"Guess we'll find out."

* * *

Pulling into the gravel lot, Jessica parked her Tahoe amidst the dusty pickups and work trucks. The vehicle looked out of place, but she couldn't help that. When she'd moved from Cleveland, it soon became apparent her sporty Camaro wasn't practical. It was a nice trade-in though, for the used four-wheel-drive SUV.

As she stepped out, the smell of hay and manure greeted her, different from the sterile office air she was used to, but in some ways, welcome. Taking a breath, she steeled herself for the conversation ahead.

She'd called the MacKays as she'd left the office, so they were expecting her.

Evan and Ethan waited on the porch. As she approached, she noted the worry etched on their faces. She climbed the steps, deciding not to mince words and be direct, and faced them both.

"I met with your mother earlier this morning."

Ethan leaned forward. "What?"

"What the hell?" Evan spit out. His expression was the most puzzling to her, sort of a mix of surprise and frustration.

"She wanted to talk about the ranch situation." Pausing, she tried to gauge their reactions. "She arrived unannounced, without an appointment," she added.

The twins stood spellbound, staring.

"Well?" Jessica prompted.

"What did she want?" Ethan asked warily.

Jessica hesitated. This wasn't going to be easy. "She wanted me to tell her what you two hadn't told her yet."

"Shit." Evan stood. "Did you?"

Gesturing with her hands and shrugging, she replied, "What could I say but the truth? I told her the struggles, the situation with the loans, and the new plan we came up with for the short term."

Ethan abruptly started pacing, agitated. "Well, perhaps you could have told her to talk to us directly? Who the hell has she been talking to...." Hastily, he moved toward the front door, jerked it open, and stuck his head inside. "Brandley!"

Unsure why Ethan was suddenly so anxious, and thinking she should deescalate the situation, Jessica stepped toward him and placed a hand on his shoulder. "Hey. Let's have a seat and talk. It's not a bad thing, really."

Ethan swung about and cried out.

Jessica jumped back, startled. "I'm so sorry!"

"Ethan!" Brandley pushed through the storm door. She glanced at Jessica. "Give us a minute." She quickly ushered her husband inside the house.

Jessica stood staring at the door.

"It's not your fault."

She turned. "What?"

"He has PSTD. Afghanistan. Navy SEAL."

"Wow. I'm so sorry. But what did I do?"

Evan took a step. "Touched him. It's okay. He gets prickly where Mom is concerned and sometimes gets overwhelmed."

"I don't know what to say."

"Let's take a walk and talk. I can fill Ethan and Brandley in later. What else did my mother say?"

He led her to the side porch. They silently took the steps down to the ground and then strolled toward the barn.

Should she tell him the rest? Maybe she shouldn't have

come at all—she was possibly crossing boundaries she shouldn't cross. Perhaps she should sugarcoat things a little and then realized that was never a good idea. "Your mother wondered if she should sell off a few acres."

Evan halted, looking gut punched. "She what? No. Not an option."

Jessica nodded. "I know it's a lot to take in. I wanted you to know what she was thinking."

"A lot to take in?" Evan exploded. "This ranch has been in our family for generations. She can't just sell it out from under us."

"She doesn't want to do that. Just a few acres."

"No. She's not thinking this through. Even a few acres will cause issues with the land to stock ratio," Evan said.

"But you've already cut back the herd."

"I know. But that doesn't leave room for growth."

Jessica nodded and let out a breath. "You're right, of course. Look. Your mother only wants what's best for the ranch and for all of you. I don't get the impression she's fully decided, but I wanted you to be prepared if she brought it up."

Ethan ran a hand over his face. Based on the earlier conversation with his mother and Noah, it appeared they had already reached a decision. "What happens now?"

Jessica wished she had an answer for him. Connie's intentions were good, but the road ahead was uncertain. "We wait for her to make another move—or you can tell her we've talked. Up to you."

* * *

Later that evening, Evan climbed the front porch steps of their mother's cabin alongside Ethan, the weight of his worries hanging heavily on his shoulders. They had agreed to hear their mother out, let her say her piece, and not share that they'd talked with Jessica.

Unless they had to.

Connie turned with a smile as they entered the kitchen, her eyes crinkling at the corners. Although a serious conversation was going to happen soon, he was very glad to see her in that kitchen puttering around.

"There you boys are. Dinner will be ready in an hour. Noah's outside with the grill."

Evan cleared his throat. "Mom, we need to talk."

"Oh?" She blinked innocently as she set a casserole dish of baked beans on the counter.

Ethan pulled out a chair for her. "Please, sit down."

With a slight sigh, Connie settled into the seat, folding her hands in her lap. "This is about the ranch, I suppose?"

"It is."

"Well then, I need Noah. One of you boys go and get him? Tell him to set those steaks aside for a minute."

"I'll go." Ethan headed out the back door.

A few minutes later, Connie and Noah sat side by side at the kitchen table, facing Ethan and Evan as they stood on the other side. Inside him, emotion churned with a mixture of determination and anxiety. He could see the strain etched in the lines on his mother's forehead, the way her knuckles were white from clasping her hands together too hard.

"Sit down, boys," she said firmly, gesturing to the chairs opposite her. "You're right. We need to talk."

Had his mother just turned the tables? Ever so slightly?

Evan glanced at his brother and took a seat, his mind racing with thoughts of impending disaster. As his thoughts rolled over the earlier conversation with Jessica, he couldn't help but feel somewhat uneasy, even though he knew she was only doing what she believed was best for all of them.

"Before we get started," Connie began, her voice wavering, "I want you both to know that I love you more than anything in this world, and I would do nothing to hurt you or this family."

"Mom, we know that." Ethan reached out to touch her hand. "But we're worried about the ranch. We've put everything into it, and now it feels like we're losing control."

"Sometimes," Connie said softly, "the hardest thing in life is knowing when to let go and trust someone else to help carry the load." She turned to face Noah, her eyes misty. "Now that Noah and I are together, we have each other to lean on. I'm not saying I don't need you boys or any of my family, because I do, but you don't have to worry about me like you did for a few years."

"Mom, we'll always worry about you."

"I know, but you don't have to." She hesitated, then took a breath. "I'm moving to Montana full time to live with Noah there. The renovations on his house are finished and, well, I just love it there, to be honest. It's our home together. I trust you both with the management of the ranch. I know you will keep me informed. Now, I need to be with my husband, and I can help Sarah with the baby."

Evan tried to understand. "So, you're not going to be here at the cabin part of the time, like you said originally?"

She shook her head. "No. I'll be here just for visits." She glanced at Noah. "You should also know I've made another decision."

While her voice remained steady, Evan noticed her hands trembled slightly.

"I'm selling the cabin and the surrounding two-hundred acres and putting the money toward the ranch debt."

The room seemed to hold its breath for a moment, the weight of Connie's words sinking in. Evan's jaw clenched, his face tightening. He looked at Ethan, who sat hunched over, searching his mother's face.

"Mom, you can't be serious," Evan finally uttered. "Dad built this cabin for you. It was a gift. The land has been in our family for generations. We can't sell it off like it doesn't matter."

"It's the best part to sell. It will bring the most money."

Evan moved and crouched in front of his mother. "Mom, no. I'll find another way."

That's when the tears sprung forth in her eyes. She cupped his face with her hands.

"Sometimes we have to make tough decisions in order to protect what we love most. I know how much this ranch means to all of us, but we're drowning, Evan. You're exhausted. I know you can't keep going on like this."

As she spoke, Evan felt respect for his mother's unwavering determination. She would risk everything to protect the land they all loved so dearly—but more than that, her family. If nothing else, he owed it to her to hear her out. But as he looked into her tired, hopeful eyes, he knew they were entering uncharted territory, and there was no telling where it might lead.

"You didn't even discuss it with us first," Evan said, unable to keep the hurt from his voice. "Jessica came by this afternoon."

"Well, then you already knew. I'm sorry. I just want to take this burden off your shoulders."

"We don't need you to protect us," Ethan said. "We're all adults here. Big decisions should be made together."

"You're right, of course." She patted Ethan's hand, then sat back with a weary smile. "Your father entrusted this land to me. It became my responsibility when Hap died. Oh, I know you two have been running it the past few years, and in our hearts, it belongs to all of us, but it's my name on the deeds and on the loans."

Ethan stood, looking down at Evan. "She's right. That's a lot of pressure on her, and honestly, I hadn't considered that."

How had he not seen? "True. And I don't want that. It's just—"

Connie put up a hand. "I can't stand seeing you boys struggle any longer. I've made my decision."

The depth of his mother's love and sacrifice was humbling. Evan grasped her hand and squeezed it. "Just one question. Did Jessica Chase have anything to do with swaying you to sell this piece of land?"

The look on Connie's face was pretty much his answer.

"Heavens no, Evan. I didn't even know the woman before I stepped into her office at the bank. I assumed David Morrow was still our loan manager."

"I see."

But Connie wasn't sure he did, evidently. She rose and stepped closer to Evan. "Look, it doesn't matter who the loan officer is, the problem is the same. But this young woman knows her stuff and I trust her. Don't give her a hard time. Do you hear me?"

After a moment, he nodded. "Yes. I hear you."

"Good. I think she can help us."

"Well, time will tell on that," Evan said gruffly. "But no more going behind our backs. We're in this as a family."

Connie nodded, dashing away a tear. "You're right. I'm sorry I didn't talk to you first."

Noah cleared his throat. "Now, you boys know I will not interfere. This is Connie's decision to make, but I am here to give advice. I will only say this for you to consider, from a man who has managed a lot of ranches in his time. From a financial standpoint, selling part of the ranch could provide the capital needed to invest in improvements and pay off debts," he said carefully, trying to keep his voice neutral. "It's not a simple choice, not by a long shot. But it might be the most practical one."

Evan faced his mother, a mix of anguish and resolve racing over his chest. "If this is what you truly believe is best, then I support that. But promise me you won't go through with this decision unless it's absolutely necessary. And you'll make no permanent moves without talking with Ethan and me."

He looked at his brother, who nodded his agreement.

"Of course." Connie grasped her son's hand. "I only want what's best for everyone. I promise you that."

Chapter Six

Jessica took a deep breath before pushing through the glass door of the conference room and stepping inside. She was not looking forward to this meeting with Connie MacKay Parker. Ever since the matriarch had announced her intention to sell a part of Sweet Grass Ranch, she had feared tensions between the family and the bank would escalate.

She'd not spoken with Evan or Connie since she'd gone to the ranch a few days earlier. Worried that she'd crossed boundaries, she had stayed away, with the idea of letting them come to her, if they needed something.

Well, that day was here. Connie had scheduled the appointment yesterday. She'd not heard from Evan.

Clutching the ranch file in her arm, she pushed through the door. Connie was already seated in the meeting room, back ramrod straight, hands folded neatly on the table. She appeared calm, if not resolved.

"Mrs. MacKay," Jessica said briskly, taking the seat across from her. "So good to see you today. What can I do for you?"

"Hi Jessica. It's Parker now." Connie smiled.

"Oh yes. I'm so sorry."

"No worries." She patted Jessica's hand on the table. "I'm eager to get things moving. We have a few things to discuss."

Jessica nodded, shuffling through the paperwork detailing the ranch's debts and assets.

Connie's gaze followed her every move. "I want to know, before we move forward with an actual sale, that things will calm down for a while. Will this sale provide the needed capital and give the boys enough time to recover and keep the rest of the ranch? Will it buy us more time to get things right?"

Pausing her shuffling, Jessica gave Connie her full attention. She could sense her apprehension and concern—and rightfully so. Selling was never easy, especially when people felt forced into it. "I understand your worry, Mrs. MacKay, er, Parker. That's a reasonable request. Just so you know, we've talked in-house with the loan committee about this solution and so far, it's all looking agreeable with the bank. But I want to make sure you understand the full ramifications of selling your property."

She paused again, studying Connie's facial expressions.

"Go on."

Jessica glanced down at the paperwork detailing the ranch's landholdings. The part Connie wanted to sell was a substantial parcel, over two-hundred acres of prime real estate nestled against the mountains. The log cabin would add even more value.

Taking a breath, she met Connie's expectant gaze. "Based on what you've told me, your property could bring in a signifi-cant amount of money. Enough to pay down a good portion of the outstanding loans. While it will create an infusion of capital, it may not be enough to resolve the outstanding debt in full, but close. I just have to see how much the parcel will sell for."

"I see."

"Is that still the direction you want to go?"

Connie's gaze bore into hers. "I'm not sure I have a choice."

Jessica nodded. "I'll send someone out to assess the property value later in the week."

"How long will this sale help matters? Have you crunched the numbers?"

"I have. The sale should satisfy enough of the outstanding loans and give your sons cash flow for about eighteen months."

"With any luck, they can turn things around in that time frame."

"Hopefully, but the ranch will not be out of the woods yet." Jessica reached out and touched Connie's hand. "Are you ready to move forward?"

Connie made direct eye contact. "Yes. I appreciate your concern, but I've given this a great deal of thought. This ranch means everything to my family. I would rather sell a small portion of it now, than have to sell the entire thing down the road. I won't stand by while it slips away."

Jessica proceeded gently. "Have you discussed this with Evan and Ethan?"

At that, Connie faltered briefly before firming her jaw. "I have. It's an emotional issue for them, even if they are letting on like it isn't, but they understand. As their mother, it's my job to make the tough choices, especially when they can't."

Jessica saw the flicker of pain in Connie's eyes and felt an unexpected surge of empathy for the burden she bore.

"I understand this is difficult," Jessica said. "You've made a brave decision. We'll make sure it counts."

Connie gave her a small, grateful smile. In that moment, it seemed an unspoken understanding had passed between the two women. "But is it a step in the right direction?"

"It is," Jessica affirmed. She appreciated Connie's pragmatism. The woman clearly understood there were no easy fixes.

"I can refer you to a real estate agent or you may have

someone in mind. I'll call you as soon as I have solid numbers," Jessica promised.

"That would be wonderful." Relief etched Connie's face.

Jessica smiled. "We're in this together, now. I want you to know you can count on me."

Connie reached across and squeezed her hand. "Thank you, Jessica. For everything." Rising, she headed for the door, then turned back. "Oh. We're having a BBQ tomorrow night. Just family and a few neighbors. Last hurrah before the snow flies. Why don't you come by?"

Her immediate thought was to keep her distance. "Oh, I'm not sure I should."

"Nonsense. Come by and see the cabin and grab a hamburger, too. I guarantee you'll love the beef." Connie grinned.

Jessica teetered on the verge of caving in. What could it hurt? "How can I say no to South Dakota beef?"

Connie gave her a hug. "You can't. See you around six."

* * *

The next evening, Evan stood at the barbecue grill, flipping steaks and burgers as smoke billowed up into the clear blue sky. The familiar smells of charcoal, wood chips, and sizzling meat filled the air, transporting him back to countless childhood summer days spent on the ranch with family.

A few neighbors had gathered, some making their way over to his mom's cabin on horseback, and others by truck or SUV. Their children were ducking in and out of barns and outbuildings, playing hide-and-seek, while the adults gravitated to the coolers of beer and pop.

Aaron and Aiden, back from Denver, laughed and joked as they set up tables in the shade of the cottonwoods. Even his serious middle brother, Dylan, cracked a smile as he appeared from the ranch house, arms loaded with an over-large bowl of potato salad and two bags of chips.

"Got your hands full there, Dylan. Need help?" Evan flipped another burger and tossed his brother a grin.

"Naw, I'm good. Heading to the tables as soon as the slow poke rodeo boys get them set up."

Evan laughed. "Hey, they are working, so don't knock it."

"I hear they are going to be pulling their weight more soon."

Nodding, Evan said, "Yes. We're in the process of selling out the rodeo stock business. I need to catch you up on a few things later tonight."

"Sounds good. Well, I'm going to get these settled over there."

Evan watched him step away, bantering with the younger brothers. It did his heart good to have everyone back at the ranch, if only for a little while. Well, almost everyone. Sarah and her husband, Cole, weren't able to make it.

Things had been mighty tough since their dad passed, but seeing his mom's eyes light up as she fussed over her boys eased some of the weight from his shoulders. Plus, she sure seemed to be head-over-heels for Noah, and that was alright by him.

Everyone needed someone to love.

"Well, look at you, flipping those burgers." His mother stepped up, smiling. "Goodness, more people showed up than I thought. Good thing we asked everyone to bring a dish. Think we have enough meat?"

Evan snorted. "Mom, we'll be eating leftover hamburgers for days."

"That's fine by me."

"No complaints here."

Connie turned toward the house, then back again. "Oh.

Jessica's due any minute," Connie said. "Be on your best behavior, now. Alright?"

Evan nodded, though his jaw tightened at the mention of the banker who held the fate of their ranch in her manicured hands. "You know I don't have anything against her."

"She's trying to help, son."

"I know. I just need to trust her. I mean, look at her. What does she know about ranches?"

"I imagine she knows more than you are giving her credit. Cattlemens wouldn't have hired her or given her our account unless they thought she knew what she was doing. I trust the bank, and therefore I trust her."

"I suppose. It's just those heels and the suits and her hair all swept up in that knot on her head, and her shaped fingernails— she doesn't look like a rancher."

Connie stepped back and peered at him, mouth open. "Does she have to? My God, Evan, what century are you living in?"

"I, uh...."

"Yes, she is pretty. That's for certain. And smart. Did you see those degrees on her office wall?"

That's not what he expected her to say. "I did."

"Brains and beauty, it seems. Give her a chance?"

"Fine, Mom."

Connie stared, smiling. "You like her."

Evan jerked his gaze up to meet hers. "What?"

"You like her. Don't you?"

"Mom...."

Grinning, she turned away, heading back to the house. Then, abruptly, she whirled back, taking several quick steps toward him. "You've been waiting a long time for the right woman, Evan MacKay. And you've put off dating so you could take care of this ranch, and all of us. I'm just saying. Maybe it's time for you to pay attention to your own life."

"Mom. Stop."

Laughing, she headed off again, waving to someone coming down the hill on horseback.

Ridiculous.

Wasn't it?

Still, he grinned inwardly as the familiar black Tahoe pulled up the dirt drive, trailed by a cloud of dust. His mom was right about one thing. Jessica looked pretty as a picture climbing out of that vehicle in her flowy sundress and big sunglasses. He couldn't help himself when he put down the spatula and headed over to her vehicle to greet her.

"Ms. Chase," he said, touching the brim of his hat. "Glad you could make it." His politeness sounded hollow to his own ears, but he had to try.

Jessica flashed a bright smile. "Please, call me Jessica. I'm not here on business."

"Fine. Call me Evan."

"So, you're the chef, Evan?"

He laughed. "I can flip a mean burger." Then leaning in closer, he whispered. "You're not one of those vegan types, are you?"

At that, Jessica laughed too. "Me? Heck no. I'm a carnivore! Now, where can I put this slaw? We should keep it cold for a while."

Evan pointed to the tables. "There are some coolers over there. See those two lanky young guys? That's Aiden and Aaron, my little brothers. Why don't you introduce yourself? They can show you where the cold foods go."

She flashed him a smile. "I will do that, Evan. Thanks. See you later."

With that, she was off. Evan returned to the grill. But admittedly, Jessica was never far from his gaze, wherever she floated off to in that pretty yellow dress and sandals.

She laughed, cackling at one of Aaron's jokes. And as she threw back her head, long hair spilling over her shoulders, he thought about what his mother had said a few minutes earlier. She was right—he'd never found a woman he'd wanted to share his life with, although he'd come close a time or two. Things always happened. The past few years, he was too busy solving the ranch's problems to focus on his love life.

Was it time for a change in that direction, too?

He watched Jessica give Noah a casual hug when she said hello to his mom. When Dylan approached, introduced himself, and held her hand a mite too long as he shook it, the green-eyed monster inside Evan reared his head a little. *What the hell?*

Then Ethan and Brandley came out of the cabin, and Brandley escorted Jessica away to somewhere. Probably to see the baby.

He'd long given up on having a woman in his life. Had he been waiting for Jessica?

Brains and beauty.

No denying she intrigued him. Had he mistaken that intrigue for mistrust? The thought made his traitorous heart skip a beat.

He wished he could read her mind, know her motives. Deep down, he wanted to trust her. In fact, it wasn't about her at all—she was really just the messenger—it was about letting his family down.

That was it, wasn't it?

Dammit. He was the problem.

The problem wasn't the bank or Jessica. It was him.

He'd failed. Much as he tried. And Jessica was the proof of it, staring him smack in the face.

"Shit."

* * *

Evan scooted the burgers off the grill and into a long, low pan, covered them with foil, and then slipped them down in a large cooler—no ice, of course—to keep them warm. As Dylan approached with a platter of rib eyes, he wondered if they should have fired up a second grill.

Dylan set the steaks aside on a small table. "More people than I expected."

"Yeah. I was just wondering if we should have had two grills going."

"I think we can make do. You look sweaty and hot. How about you take a break and I'll cover the grill right now? You know I do steaks better."

Evan grinned. "I'll keep letting you think that."

But he welcomed a break. Stepping over to a cooler full of icy drinks, he dunked a clean dish towel down into the water, then ran it over his face and head. The cold shock not only made him feel a bit more refreshed, but cleaner.

Settling his hat back on his head and tossing the towel aside, he looked up to see a newer model Dodge Ram pickup truck with Montana plates pulling into the barn lot. Squinting against the early evening glare, he tried to make out the figure exiting from the driver's side.

Ethan stepped up. "Who's that?"

"Not sure."

The cowboy stretched, as if he'd been driving for a while, then looked toward the cabin and waved. Evan's attention moved to the couple stepping away from the porch, waving back —his mother and Noah.

"What the...?"

Dylan joined the older twins. "What's Gage Parker doing here?"

Evan had to think a minute about who Gage Parker was. "Isn't he Noah's nephew?"

"I think so," Ethan responded.

Dylan shoved back his hat. "He is. Parker and Callie Rankin are his cousins. You might also remember he is Cole's boss."

That's right. Cole was Sarah's husband. "Ah. The hotel billionaire. Right?"

"And he's been buying up a lot of ranches lately, I understand," Dylan added.

Ethan and Evan stared.

"How do you know so much?" Ethan asked.

"I talk with the Rankins occasionally. Besides, I was just in Billings the past couple of weeks, and I had dinner with Cole and Sarah a few times. Gage is one big deal in that neck of the woods."

Evan stared. "Then what the hell is he doing in *our* neck of the woods?"

All three brothers directed their attention to the billionaire rancher, who stood chatting and smiling with their mother and Noah, as they steadily made their way toward the trio.

Every muscle in Evan's body tensed.

Chapter Seven

Connie's demeanor seemed to perk up as the three of them headed her way. Evan detected some level of excitement in her voice. "Boys! You remember Gage Parker?"

The brothers halted all at once, looking over the well-dressed cowboy. Evan opted for indifference.

Dylan smiled and tipped his head. "Gage. Nice to see you again." He offered his hand.

Gage shook it. "I enjoyed our dinner the other evening with Sarah and Cole in Billings."

"Yes, that was nice."

Ethan and Evan exchanged glances but remained silent.

So, was this billionaire rancher there because of Dylan? What did he say to him? Evan eyed his middle brother.

Gage put out his hand again to the pair, shaking them quickly. "Sorry to drop in unannounced. I was in the neighborhood. Heard so much about Sweet Grass Ranch over the years, and now that you all are family—thanks to your mom and my Uncle Noah here—I felt it high time I visit."

Ethan shot Evan a wary look. They both knew Gage

showing up was no coincidence. "Just in time for barbecue," he offered.

"Gage." Evan leveled his gaze at the man. "To what do we owe the pleasure?"

"Cuts right to the chase. I like that." Gage's smile didn't reach his eyes, though. "To be honest, I have a business proposition for you boys, if you will hear me out."

Evan kicked up a clump of dirt. "And what kind of business proposition would that be?"

"Why don't we take a walk, just the three of us?" Gage directed his request at Evan and Ethan. "I'd love to see more of this beautiful ranch of yours."

The last thing Evan wanted was to go anywhere with him. "Sure," he ground out. "We could do that, but I need to stay close to the grill, and besides, I think Mom needs to be in on this discussion." He gave his mother a quick look. He wasn't sure what was happening. Had his mother instigated this? Noah? Dylan, or perhaps Sarah? "Let's all sit on the porch."

"I think that's a fine idea," Connie said. She took Noah's arm. "There are plenty of empty chairs."

Dylan interrupted. "You all do that. I need to get back to the grill and steaks."

"Sure thing, Dylan," Gage said. "Hope to see you again soon."

Dylan touched the brim of his hat and nodded. "Of course."

As they ambled toward the porch, Evan watched Dylan walk away. If he had started something in Billings, he wouldn't walk away from the discussion now. Would he?

Gage casually bantered with their mother and Noah as they walked in front of Evan and Ethan. After settling into chairs on the porch, Gage got right to the point, directing his attention to Evan and Ethan. He sat directly across from them on the edge of the wooden rocker, leaning their way, his elbows on his knees and his hands tented.

"Uncle Noah mentioned that you boys were struggling right now. I'm in a position to help."

Evan noisily huffed out a breath and looked off. *Coming in here from out of state and thinking you can....*

Ethan touched his knee, directing his attention back to Gage.

"Go on."

His mother's eyes held a worried expression.

"I've been looking at South Dakota ranches for a while, branching out beyond Montana. But I'm a picky buyer and I know what I want. I know you've considered selling this cabin and some surrounding acreage. I will tell you right now, I'll give you your price for it." He looked at Connie.

"Oh, my!" His mother's words burst from her mouth. Her eyes teared up as she met Evan's gaze.

There it was. The billionaire cowboy knew about the possible sale, so the culprit was his mother, or maybe Noah. Evan tensed, his worst fears confirmed. Gage wanted their land.

"In fact," Gage continued lightly, "I'd be willing to buy the whole ranch. Lock, stock, and barrel, if you want to discuss."

Evan shot up. "The ranch isn't for sale."

Gage held up his hands. "Now just hear me out."

Crossing his arms, Evan's jaw clenched. Nothing this fancy cowboy said would make him consider selling their legacy. Not to him. Who the hell was he, anyway? Some rich cowboy who collected ranches and hotels like they were baseball cards?

Evan stared stonily at Gage.

Never.

Ethan sat beside him, alarmingly quiet, then said, "Sit down, Evan. Hear him out."

Was his brother even considering the offer?

Evan sat uncomfortably on the edge of his seat. "This is not something I want to hear out, I'll be honest. But have at it." He eyed Gage Parker.

The cowboy met his gaze with eyes that meant business. "There are several ways we could work a sale. I could buy you out in full, in cash, or we could cut a deal where you boys would keep running the place," Gage continued. "You clearly know what you're doing. The house and barns and equipment could remain yours—I don't want to take your home. I'd just provide the financing for the ranch, and we'd work out a split of the profits."

Ethan shifted his weight, looking at their mother.

Evan cut in sharply. "We don't need your money."

Gage raised an eyebrow. "Oh? Word around town is you're struggling to stay afloat. I can offer you financial security."

"Evan," his mother interrupted, "we should consider the offer on the cabin. I'd much rather sell to someone we know—family—than a stranger."

He noted that. She was right, but momentarily, he couldn't go there. "We'll manage."

"It's an investment in your family's future and legacy."

"Our legacy isn't for sale," Evan ground out.

Gage spread his hands. "I'm offering you a lifeline here. With my backing, you have security, keep your home, and get to live and work on this ranch for as long as any of you want. If that's the way you want to cut the deal."

"And you get our land, is that it?" Ethan challenged.

"A fair trade. Yes, the land would be mine. I assume the risks. You reap the benefits."

Evan scanned the conflicted faces of his brother and mother. Were they tempted by Gage's offer, worn down by the struggle? Could they really turn down the chance to secure their home? "Why? What's in it for you?"

Gage cleared his throat, leaning forward. "Look. I love ranching. I want to preserve the ranch lifestyle for generations to come. And of course, I'd profit from cattle sales and such. We'd work up an agreement."

His mother's eyes shimmered with unshed tears. She met his look and gave a single, firm shake of her head.

"Pride won't keep this ranch going forever, son." Gage's voice hardened slightly. "I'd like to know what your mother thinks, and the rest of your family."

"That's for us to discuss with the family, not you," Evan told him.

Connie interjected. "I'd like to hear more. And yes, we need to talk to everyone."

"I agree," Ethan added. "Gage, why don't the three of us— you, Evan, and I—head into the office and get some more details? Then later this evening, or tomorrow, depending on how long this BBQ lasts, we'll discuss with family and get back with you."

Evan wanted to refuse, but he knew Gage wouldn't leave without some sort of concession. He would fight for the ranch with his last breath. Gage Parker would not claim what was theirs. Not now, not ever.

"We appreciate your offer, Mr. Parker. But like my brother said, we can't decide on anything right now. We need to talk this out with the others. I think we have enough information for the time being."

Around him, his family nodded, bolstered by his stand.

Gage nodded his understanding and stood. Withdrawing a business card from his suit pocket, he handed it to Evan, and another to Ethan. When Evan didn't reach for his, Gage placed it on the arm of the wooden chair. "My offer will remain open. I trust you'll make the sensible choice for your family's future."

"Our future is right here." Evan swept his arm across the

landscape. "This land, this life, it's in our blood. This is not a simple discussion for any of us."

"Understood." Gage sighed and glanced around the group. "Enjoy the rest of your barbecue. I'm heading back to Montana in the morning. You know where to find me when you are ready."

Tipping his hat, Gage strode to his truck and drove away. The family stood in uneasy silence as his taillights disappeared down the drive.

Connie crossed her arms and looked directly at her sons. "As soon as the last guest leaves, gather the family inside." Then, turning, she disappeared inside the cabin.

* * *

Jessica sat alone on the back porch steps of Connie's cabin, gazing out at the sunset painting the sky in vibrant pinks and oranges. It wouldn't be long before the orb would drop fully behind the Black Hills, and night would take over.

Evan lowered himself down beside her. "Beautiful sunset."

"Like none I've ever seen before," she said.

"That's the beauty—no two are alike."

"I can definitely see why you don't want to sell this place. Every inch of this ranch is breathtaking."

She could feel his gaze on her face, perhaps studying her. What was he thinking?

"I'm glad you can see that," he said after a moment.

Jessica let out a long sigh and looked at Evan. "Long day?" He looked tired.

"Somewhat."

She nodded. "I sensed that."

"Been out here for a while?"

"Not too long. I was sitting out front earlier. On the porch."

"Ah."

Turning slightly, she caught his gaze. "I know it's not my place, but I think you made the right call, not making a snap decision with the offer you just got. This ranch is your legacy, and you are right to discuss with family first."

"You heard."

"I couldn't help but hear. I was on the porch before you came up, and once the conversation started with all of you, I didn't want to leave and interrupt, so I kept quiet."

"You have every right. The bank has a huge stake in this game."

"That's not why I stayed. I really didn't want to appear intrusive."

"I appreciate that."

Turning more fully toward him, she continued. "Look, Evan. Money is my business. Selling the entire ranch, well, I'm just not sure that's the right direction to go. Money comes and goes, but land... Land is forever." She paused and searched his eyes. "And I'm not advising you right now as your banker. I'm talking to you as a friend."

Friend? When did that happen?

He blinked at her words, studying her face.

"Yeah, well, forever doesn't pay the bank." Evan grinned and rested his elbows on his knees. "I just wish I knew what to do. We're barely scraping by as it is."

"You'll figure it out. You and your family."

Evan met her gaze. She sensed being vulnerable was diffi-cult for him. Would he open up to her? Did she want him to?

"It's not just the money," he admitted. "I feel like I've let everyone down. Like I failed my family, my heritage. And I know I've acted badly around you, Jessica. I want you to know it wasn't you. All you want to do is help us see this through. I realized today that it's my fear of failure that was making me rather... Shall we say, prickly?"

Hearing that made her smile. "Prickly, huh? Maybe grumpy, or perhaps even angry?" She nudged him playfully. "Alright, prickly is a good word."

A slow sideways grin broke across his face. "Just call me the prickly cowboy."

"Will do." Jessica placed a hand on his arm. "Evan, you could never fail your family. Or yourself. All you've done is give your heart and soul to this place. No one could ask for more."

His expression softened, and Jessica watched his gaze drift from her eyes to her mouth.

Caught in the moment's intimacy, she parted her lips slightly, an involuntary invitation, she guessed. Did she want him to kiss her?

Did he want to?

Evan tentatively leaned closer, his gaze locked on her lips.

Her eyes fluttered closed. Their kiss was tentative at first, a soft nibble and slow brushing together, then deepened as she pressed in closer. The kiss hung in the air between them for a small eternity, their lips softly touching, breaths mingling.

After a moment, Evan pulled back, putting some space between them—his gaze tangling with hers. "I'm sorry, I shouldn't have done that. I don't know what came over me. I was way out of line and—"

"No. Don't apologize."

He started to stand.

"Stop, Evan." She grasped his hand. "It's okay. I... We probably shouldn't have kissed, but... I'm not sorry."

He settled back down. "You're not?"

"No. In fact, I wouldn't object if you kissed me again."

By the startled look on his face, she knew she'd taken things too far. *Time to back up here.* "But since I am your financial advisor, that would complicate things, wouldn't it? It's probably best we don't."

Geez, Jessica. That was a load of mixed messages....

"Of course." Evan agreed. "You're right. I don't want you to feel pressured. Your job comes first."

"The ranch comes first."

Suddenly, her heart ached with the lure of more, and the reality of potential loss.

She gave him a half smile that felt rather bittersweet and added. "It has to come first. I don't want to do anything to risk..." She trailed off, opposing sentiments playing over her heart. "Maybe once all this is through...."

Stop. Best leave this alone.

Behind them, the screen door creaked open, and a group of giggling pre-teen girls raced out and across the barn lot. Voices of family members drifted out from inside the house, shattering the intimate spell.

Evan stood, extending his hand to help Jessica up. "We'd better get back to the barbecue. Looks like people are leaving and I suppose I should round up my family soon for the discussion."

"Of course."

He gave her a quick grin and tugged her to her feet. Her body rested slightly against his, their chests colliding. Their eyes met once more, a silent promise of something more passing between them.

Evan slowly released her fingers, but their gazes held. "I'm going to head over toward the tables, talk to a few people." He murmured, then took a step down. "See you soon."

"Let me know how it goes with the family."

He nodded and turned.

Jessica took a deep breath and watched Evan stroll away. His broad shoulders rippled and stretched the worn denim of his shirt, years of obvious physical labor etched into his tall, fit frame. His firm hands, leathered and calloused, comforted her as he'd held them. She'd held many a rough cowboy hand over her young life, particularly her father's and grandfather's.

This prickly cowboy was rapidly warming her heart. He not only reminded her of a life she'd loved so long ago, but was helping her get back to her roots—roots she'd let go of for far too long.

Stepping away from the porch, she intentionally moved in the opposite direction. The heels of her sandals sank into the soft dirt with each step—a sensation she found rather familiar and nostalgic, so different from the paved city streets and concrete sidewalks. But she didn't mind. There was something comforting about this rugged land that called to a long-forgotten part of her.

Her gaze lifted as she wandered away, falling into the nostalgia of the moment, the sun quickly slipping behind the Black Hills to the west.

As a young girl, she'd grown up on a similar ranch, until hard times had fallen on her parents. After their ranch sold, and her family had moved to Cheyenne, she'd spent her summers on her grandparents' ranch, riding horses and helping with chores. It was there she first fell in love with the freedom and spirit of the wide-open plains.

You wouldn't find her in the house doing chores unless her grandmother insisted. Instead, she preferred mucking the stalls, feeding, and brushing the horses.

That ranch was the land she'd grown to love, had busted her butt on when she'd been thrown, had tasted when she'd fallen face first into the dust.

But when her mom got sick and her dad got a little crazy, those days ended abruptly. The summer she turned fourteen, her life changed forever.

Over the years, she'd buried her remembrances of ranch life deep. She built a new life, new dreams. Yet, standing there with the taste of dust on her tongue, and the last of the sunset warming her face, and a handsome cowboy walking away from her, she felt a pang for all she had left behind—for a life she may have missed.

Abruptly, she twisted back, searching for Evan.

She didn't want him to have regrets. Not like her. How could she tell him not to sell the ranch?

I can't. It's not my place.

As if he knew she was looking, Evan turned back, too, and met her gaze. She imagined his eyes creasing slightly, and she was sure he offered her a rare, crooked smile, although he was almost too far away to tell.

Still, her heart stuttered.

"Time to go home," she said softly.

Turning, she headed for her SUV, Evan's kiss tucked away into a secret place in her heart.

* * *

Evan watched Jessica's taillights fade as she traveled out the ranch road. With a sigh, he turned to Ethan and Dylan. "Time to gather the family."

"Let's get Sarah on the phone," Dylan said.

"Good idea." Evan nodded.

"I'll get Brandley and the boys," Ethan offered, "If you can find mom and Noah. They may still be inside."

Over the next few minutes, the family drifted into the cabin and settled into the great room. Noah and Connie were indeed already there. Evan couldn't help but notice that his mother may have been crying.

He settled himself on an ottoman, perched on the edge, and looked over his family. "This is not easy."

Immediately, everyone's attention was on him.

"Evan," his mother interrupted. "Let me. This is my job."

Straightening up, he met his mother's gaze and held it. "Alright."

Connie rose and stood behind Noah's chair, placing her hands on his shoulders. One of Noah's hands covered hers protectively.

"I'm going to be brief and then you all can talk. Sarah is on the phone, right?"

"I'm here, Mom," Sarah called out from the speaker.

"Good. Because I think I can only do this once."

Aiden blew out a breath. "Oh hell. Are you sick?"

She shook her head. "No, no. Nothing like that." Glancing around the group, she paused. "No easy way to say this, like Evan said. You all know the ranch is in trouble. Hap, well, he didn't leave things in a good place. We're not blaming him, of course, but things could have been fixed long ago if he'd paid closer attention, however...."

She stopped, let out a long breath, then continued.

"Not here to beat that dead horse. However, since then, Evan and Ethan have managed the bank plan made last year, and Dylan has been here working as much as he could spare, and Aiden and Aaron have worked hard at the stock business except it just couldn't get off the ground, and Sarah has contributed money too, with her concert fundraiser last year. You've all worked hard. But unfortunately, it's not enough."

"What is it, Mom?" Aaron stood, stepping closer to her. "Just say it."

Connie lifted her chin. "It's my turn to contribute. I'm selling the cabin and two hundred acres."

"No!" Sarah's shout came from the phone. "Mom! Dad built that cabin for you."

"Yes, he did. And likely, the expense of this cabin was one thing that put us in debt. I have to sell it. I've already talked at length with the bank, and things are in motion."

"Where will you live?" Dylan asked.

"With Noah, of course, over at Rock Creek."

They all stayed silent for a moment. Evan knew it wasn't like they hadn't already suspected that she would, but Rock Creek Ranch was hours away in Montana.

"There is more," she went on. "Gage Parker has offered to buy this piece of land. I'm inclined to accept his offer because he's family. I'm grateful, to tell you the truth, but I'm unsure how he knew about the potential sale. Anyone want to fess up?"

The phone crackled, and a baby cried from the other end. "Sorry, Mom," Sarah said. "That was me. I let it slip the other night at dinner."

Dylan interrupted. "And I did too. We shared a bit of info with Gage, and if that wasn't okay, then I apologize."

Evan shook his head. "Well, that question is answered."

Connie caught his eye. "And that's okay," she added. "Now we know. I was afraid the rumor mill had spread all the way to Montana." She glanced about, pausing. "So, the other news... Also, this afternoon, we had an offer to buy the entire ranch."

Saying the words must have been the final straw for her, because his mother faltered and started to go down, clutching Noah's shoulders. Evan jerked to his feet. "Mom!"

He rushed forward and helped her back to her seat. Noah put his arms around her and held her. "It's alright, Connie," he crooned. "This is going to be alright."

Evan knew he had to continue. He squared himself and looked over at his family. "Look. You may have seen Gage Parker here this afternoon. He made us an offer for the ranch.

We could sell outright or cut a deal where we keep the house and run the ranch. He foots the bills."

"And he gets the ranch?" Aaron asked.

"Yes. We get the security of living here and working here."

"Like hired hands." Aaron looked off with disgust.

"Well, ain't that just shit." Aiden shot up and walked out the back door. Aaron silently followed.

"I don't know what to say," Sarah said quietly from the phone. "The baby's crying, so I'm going to hang up and think about this."

"We'll call you tomorrow, Sarah."

That left Dylan, Ethan, and Evan in the room with their mother and Noah.

"This is hard on them," Connie said.

"It's hard on all of us, Mom. We've just had more time to deal with it."

She patted Noah on the leg. "I think I want a bath and then bed."

Noah nodded. "You go on up. I'll be there soon."

Evan watched his mother slowly move up the stairs. "She okay?" he asked Noah.

"This has taken a toll."

"I know."

Noah leaned closer to the boys, clearing his throat. "I want to say something. Take Gage's offer only if it is the right thing to do. I'm not going to weigh in one way or the other. While this is a family decision, and I hope I am family, I feel like I should remain neutral. I've not been in this family long enough to have a vote. Just know that whatever you and your mother decide, however you decide it, you have my support."

Evan thought about that for a moment. "You know, in some ways, I want you to have an opinion. Like Dad would have had.

I know you are not Dad, but it's like I want someone else to make this decision and just tell me what to do."

Noah reached out and touched Evan's hand. "Now you're the one looking to decide. You're the dad—you and Ethan, too. Make it because Connie can't. She's too emotionally involved. She needs you boys to make this decision. Do it for her."

Evan looked at Ethan and Dylan, their faces somber. Dylan said, "It's up to the three of us. Can we agree on that?"

Ethan nodded. "Yes."

Abruptly, Evan felt his shoulders fall and a huge relief wash over him. "Yes. I can't do this alone, either. The three of us."

Chapter Eight

While he knew he should consider Gage Parker's offer, Evan couldn't keep his mind off Jessica. Her soft lips tasted like honey and lured him in like a fine whiskey—and he wasn't much of a drinker, but that's all he could think of as he'd brushed his mouth over hers.

This is how fine whiskey should taste—sweet, soft, subtle, sophisticated. Warm and sexy....

She was complicated enough to rival the finest bourbon. But who was he to think he could be with her? Rough, old, grumpy cowboy that he was.

Crossing his arms over the fence, he surveyed the open grassland. The late morning sun cast long shadows across the rugged hills, highlighting their deep ridges and valleys. His emotions were playing hide-and-seek, too—dipping into shadowy and dangerous territories as far as the ranch was concerned but teased into the light when he thought of Jessica.

The crunch of tires on gravel broke his musings. Reluctantly, he tucked the memory of Jessica's kiss into a corner of his mind.

A dusty pickup pulled up the drive. He recognized it

instantly—their neighbor, Nate Brave Eagle. Evan watched as Nate stepped out, tall and fit in worn jeans and boots. His long black hair was tied back into a braid.

"Evan," Nate called out, smiling.

"How are you, Nate? What brings you by?"

Nate approached slowly, his dark eyes scanning the landscape. He was of the Oglala Lakota Sioux Tribe on the nearby Pine Ridge Reservation, but he lived on a ranch he'd bought years back that neighbored Sweet Grass. Nate's father was White, or as the locals say, Anglo. His mother, Lakota. Nate had grown up in both worlds, spending time in Rapid City with his dad and with his mother on the reservation. Over the years, Nate had become more traditional in his ways. Besides ranching, he'd taken the half-time position of culture teacher at Swift Horse Elementary School.

"Came by to talk to you and Ethan. Got an idea."

Evan tensed. Nate meant well, he knew, but... Had word gotten around about their problems? "We're doing just fine here, Nate," he said gruffly.

"I know, I know," Nate replied. "But with the cattle issues lately, seems you could use some extra income. I want to propose a partnership."

Evan frowned, unsure. A shadow passed over Nate's face as he continued. "You know I have a buffalo herd and I've been selling the meat online. I literally cannot keep up with the demand. Bottom line is, I want to expand the herd, but I need more grazing land. Thought maybe we could work together, lease part of your ranch."

Evan stared at the hills, picturing them filled with buffalo. It didn't seem right, but why couldn't it? Bison roamed the hills for centuries. Nate could be on to something. They both had mutual interests in the land, and Evan respected Nate's devotion to his culture and traditional ways, as well as conservationism. "Nate, I don't know. I think I need more information. Not saying no, but...."

Ethan appeared from the barn and shouted. "Hey, Nate!"

Evan motioned him over. "You want to hear this."

"Oh? What's up?"

Nate tipped his head toward Ethan. "I think we should go into business together. Make no mistake, I've heard the rumors. The more I thought about it, the more I realized we might help each other out." He shared his idea with Ethan.

Evan watched his brother's eyes light up at the idea. Still, Evan wasn't certain. Maybe he should add skeptical to the list of descriptors he was becoming.

Grumpy, prickly, skeptical cowboy....

"Let me tell you more about my philosophy and how I run my business, and then you can decide if you want to partner."

"Sure thing, Nate. Let's hear it."

Nate settled against the fence. "I practice cultural ways as much as possible. We do what they call a humane field harvest. I believe the buffalo should have ample room to range and roam, and then provide them the dignity of death on the prairie where they grazed. We do not trailer them off to a feedlot to be killed and butchered. We do everything right here on the land."

Ethan nodded. "I've seen your tractor-trailer rigs for harvest. Impressive."

"We will need to invest in another couple of units if we expand the herd—but that's down the road, and we can talk about your involvement then."

Ethan stepped closer. "What about feeding?"

"We prairie graze. No feed. Our herds are one-hundred-percent grass fed. The grazing is also good for the land and soil, which continue to produce more grass annually."

"So, the meat is all organic?"

"Yes. No grains, no hormones, or antibiotics. Non-

GMO. No herbicides or pesticides. There is a growing market for this kind of meat. My customer base is increasing steadily."

Evan and Ethan exchanged glances.

"I can see it," Ethan finally said, rubbing the stubble on his chin. "We both respect the land. Keeping the old ways, trying to heal the damage done to the prairie over the years. Plus, the creek runs through both our ranches, so we've an excellent water source."

"And we provide high-quality, healthy meat to consumers." Nate nodded, a glimmer of hope in his eyes. "Bison are part of this land, part of who we are as Native people and ranchers. They help to restore the balance we've lost." He eyed the brothers. "Maybe they could help restore the balance of things here at Sweet Grass, too."

Evan glanced at Ethan, who was listening intently. His brother had always been more open to change than him.

"And you'd be helping us out," Ethan added. "With cattle prices so low, we could cull the cattle herd even more, reallocate land, and focus more on bison."

"Except we know nothing about bison," Evan interjected.

"But I do." Nate grinned. "There are things to consider. We'd need more secure fencing to keep the cattle and bison separate. There is no brucellosis in my herd, and I intend to keep it that way—but we have to be careful, if you decide to keep a cattle herd, too."

Evan exhaled, feeling the weight of responsibility for the ranch and his family. He knew they were struggling, and while the idea was intriguing, were they surrendering a part of who they were to Nate and his ideals?

Nate seemed to sense his turmoil and placed a hand on Evan's shoulder. "Look. I don't aim to take anything away from you. Just want to work together, side by side, to keep this land thriving to better us both. This land—it's in my blood, same as yours."

Looking at Nate, Evan saw the truth of it. This man loved the land as much as he did, and he was offering them a chance to survive. An alternative to Gage Parker's proposal.

"Alright," Evan finally said. "Let's take it to the family. We have to discuss with them, Nate." Once again, they were going to have to call a family meeting.

"That's all I ask." Relief flooded Nate's face. "This could be a beneficial partnership for both of us."

Evan knew he had to say one more thing. "Nate, you should know that we've had an offer to buy the entire ranch. We don't think that's the way we want to go, but the family is still discussing that option, too. You've given us something more to consider. Just want you to know that."

Nate gave him a teasing grin. "I already knew about that," he chuckled. "Why do you think I hightailed myself over here this morning? That cowboy from Montana stopped me on the road yesterday, asking for directions to Sweet Grass."

"He told you he wanted to buy our ranch?"

Nate grinned. "He indicated he was in the market to buy a ranch around here. I put two and two together."

Slightly relieved, Evan said, "I'll call you in the morning, Nate. Thanks for stopping by."

"Of course."

The men shook hands—the possibility of a future passing between them.

* * *

"Nate Brave Eagle came by today with an interesting idea."

Evan stood with his back to the fireplace, hands in his pockets. They'd all gathered after dinner in the living room of his mother's cabin. His brothers, and his mother and Noah, sat looking back at him. Sarah couldn't make the call.

"Oh? How is he? Been forever since I've seen him." Connie sat up straighter, her eyes bright with curiosity. "What did he want?"

Evan cleared his throat. "A partnership. We need to work out the details, but there is no use doing that until we all agree. He wants to lease part of our land for his bison business, and possibly share in his business model down the road. Says it would be more profitable than cattle right now."

"Bison? He has a large operation over there, doesn't he?"

"And does a good business."

Noah angled closer. "I've seen some good ranches ruined by bison, and others profit. How is his business currently?"

Evan noted the older rancher's comment. It didn't surprise him. Bison had gotten a bad rap among cattle ranchers for generations past—but that attitude had shifted somewhat. "Appears his business is solid, and we like his business model. We would need to dig into the details further with him, but it appears he's doing very well."

Noah nodded and sat back, glancing at Connie.

"We'd have to make some changes," Ethan explained. "Rotate the cattle to separate pastures, reinforce the fences, likely reduce the cattle herd even more than we had planned."

Aaron shifted his stance, his brow furrowed. "What about disease? Bison are prone to brucellosis, aren't they? Wouldn't that put our herd at risk?"

"That's a concern. Something we'll have to manage carefully."

"But Nate thinks it's worth trying," Ethan added. "And frankly, we could use the money from the land lease."

"How long would it take for a profit?" Dylan stood, approaching Evan.

"That's a discussion we still need to have, and likely, with the bank, too. Jessica and I discussed renegotiating some leases now that the cattle numbers are down, but this is different, I suppose." The thought of discussing a new possibility with her troubled him. What would she think?

A heavy silence fell over the room as the weight of their situation sank in.

"It's not like we have a lot of options," Aiden said.

"Actually, we have options," Connie reminded them. "We have Gage Parker's offer, too. We have choices. Sell the ranch whole hog or sell off a small part and partner with Nate."

Evan gazed out the window, watching the sunset paint ribbons of pink and orange across the endless sky. The view had been a constant his whole life, but suddenly felt impermanent.

"Selling off pieces of our land goes against everything Dad believed in," Ethan said, his voice thick with emotion. "This ranch was his whole life."

"Dad loved this place. But we can't cling to the past," Dylan said. "Maybe it's time for a change."

Evan could see the worry in his mother's eyes.

"What do you think, Mom?"

She took a deep breath. "Your father was so proud of Sweet Grass..." She paused, looking over her children. "However, it was also Hap's fault that we ended up like this. We have to be realistic. Yes, your dad loved the ranch, but maybe he didn't love it enough to save it."

Her words settled over Evan, easing the tension in his shoulders. "Maybe he didn't know how to save it, Mom."

She nodded. "Maybe not."

"So, it's up to us."

Later that evening, Evan stepped out onto the front porch, the screen door softly closing behind him. They'd left the family discussion unresolved, but he knew they had to make some decisions sooner, rather than later. Leaning against the railing, he gazed out over the ranch, the moonlight bathing the rolling hills in a soft glow.

The door creaked open behind him. Ethan crossed the porch. "I think we should give Nate's bison idea serious consideration," he said after a minute. "It could turn things around for us."

"Maybe." Evan rubbed his jaw, conflicted. "It's risky. Bison need so much space."

"But that's why he needs us. It's a win-win situation. We could make it work."

"I don't know..." Evan frowned.

Ethan leaned against the porch railing next to him. "I get it. Believe me. But we need to do something."

"It is tempting. I just wish I knew more about the business. We're cowboys, not buffalo wranglers."

"We're survivors," Ethan argued gently.

Evan fell silent, turning over his brother's words.

"Tell you what," Ethan said. "Let's sleep on it. We have time to weigh all the options before making any final decisions. We should visit Nate and see his operation. Get some more information."

As much as the uncertainty gnawed at him, Evan knew Ethan was right.

"Alright, brother," Evan said finally. "Let's sleep on it."

* * *

Long after Ethan had left with his family for the main house, Evan sat in the rocker on the porch, his jacket zipped up to his chin, and his hat over his eyes. The nights were growing cooler, but he'd settled there for a while just thinking about their options.

The porch door squeaked open, and his mother stepped out. Wearing her gown, bathrobe, and furry slippers, she sat beside him in a matching wooden rocker.

"You should get some sleep." She placed a hand over his on the chair arm.

"I will."

"Evan, I want to say something."

He met his mother's gaze, her eyes a little misty in the moonlight. "Yes?"

"You need to stop bearing this burden on your shoulders. No one faults you for anything. You carried this ranch for a long time before Hap died, and then later, when Ethan was still in the Navy. Dylan always had other interests, and the younger boys? They just want to play—although those days are numbered. It's time for them to grow up, and in some ways, the potential changes with the ranch will make them do that.

"Decisions are not yours alone to make. I know we all keep saying this, but the worry plays all over your face. The tension is bunched up on your shoulders and you can't relax. I can see all that."

"Mom...."

She put up a hand. "This is what I want you to do. Tomorrow, call Jessica. Go to the bank. Take Dylan and Ethan with you. Brandley too, if you think she can help. Tell Jessica about the two offers, and then all of you decide. You don't have to ask me, just do it. Whatever you decide, I am behind you and will support you with the others."

Evan studied his mother's face. "You're sure?"

"I'm positive. Decide tomorrow, and let's get this behind us."

Slowly, Evan nodded. "Alright."

She smiled. "Good. Now, go home and get some sleep."

He stood and pulled his mother to her feet, and then into his arms. He bear-hugged her like he'd not done in a long time. "Love you, Mom."

"I love you too, son," she whispered. "Good night."

Evan stepped back and watched her go into the house, then headed for his truck.

Chapter Nine

Evan usually took an early ride, but gave his quarter horse, Nomad, the day off. The buckskin appreciated a slow morning once in a while, just like he did. Those were few, but welcome when they came.

He pushed off the post as the crunch of gravel under tires shifted his attention. Jessica's SUV pulled into the lot between the house and barn, and she parked at the side of the house. She stepped out of her vehicle, impeccably dressed as always, in a navy suit and heels. She wore her hair down, and Evan had to admit, he liked it that way.

"Morning," he called out. "Not sure those shoes are ranch ready, but I have to say you wear them well." He met her beside her vehicle.

Jessica smiled teasingly as she approached. "I'll make do."

He wondered about her playful smile. Last they left things, seemed to him, it was all business between them.

"Thanks for coming out here. We would have come to your office."

She smiled. "I know. Easier for me, rather than all of you hiking into Rapid—especially for Ethan and Brandley with the baby. Coming out here gets me away from that stuffy environment. Besides, my calendar was open."

They stood side-by-side, surveying the pasturelands between the house and the main road. "It's so peaceful out here," Jessica said after a moment.

Evan studied her from the side, her gaze traveling over the terrain. She seemed lost in thought for a moment.

"Difficult to believe the ranch is struggling."

Evan nodded, his smile fading. "Drought's been hard on the land. And while beef is high in the stores, the cattle prices aren't what they used to be." He looked at her. "Well, you know the story. I'm not telling you anything new."

"No." She paused, catching his eye, her gaze lingering.

For a blip of a second, temptation poked at him to reach out and touch her cheek. As if she sensed the direction of his thoughts, she broke eye contact and took a step toward the house.

Ah, yes. All business. Okay.

"If it helps," she said, "you're not the only ranch suffering. Supplies are expensive and short. So many ranchers are choosing not to expand their herds right now."

So maybe the bison business isn't such a bad idea.

"You said on the phone you had another offer?"

"I did."

"Tell me more."

"Let's head inside and find Ethan and Brandley. Dylan got called into work early, so he won't be here."

"Alright."

They moved into the house and met Ethan in Hap's old office, which was where Brandley did most of her work. She rushed in a moment later with their infant son, Nolan, on her hip. The baby was babbling and crying a little. They all settled in and Evan shared Nate Brave Eagle's proposal with Jessica, while the other two listened.

Evan watched as Jessica drummed her fingers on the desk, apparently thinking.

"Nate's idea could be an interesting opportunity for you," she said. "What are your thoughts so far?"

"To be honest," Ethan replied, "I wondered if the bank would go for it. They're all about cattle. Would they approve a plan like this or think it risky?"

Jessica nodded. "There is risk, and we'd have to weigh that against the potential success of the operation. You know I have to run this up the chain, so I can't speak definitively. We need to get ducks in a row before I do that."

"Of course," Brandley interjected, shifting the baby to her other leg, and bouncing him. "I'm happy to work on that. I can meet with Nate to see what his ideas are for a partnership, financially speaking. Before you leave, let's discuss exactly what you would need." Then to the child, she whispered, "Shh. Be a good boy, sweetie...."

"That's a good idea. I'm pretty sure the bank will not lay out any more capital, so a partnership would need to be heavy on money flowing into this ranch, not the other way around. For example, Nate leasing grazing land and perhaps getting him to shore up the fencing between the herds—your cattle and his bison."

"That could be a good place to start," Ethan offered.

"I agree." Jessica nodded, smiling at Ethan. "Also, if you reduce your cattle herd, you'll have some cash flow into the ranch there, too."

"That's right," Ethan said. "I hadn't thought of that."

"Then perhaps in year two," Brandley added, "Sweet Grass could start our own bison herd."

"Yes! Brandley, that's excellent. Let's work on that plan after you and Nate talk."

Evan sensed Jessica's genuine interest as she and Brandley chatted softly. She truly wanted what was best for the ranch and his family, not just the bank's bottom line. He had garnered an unhealthy amount of mistrust with the bank the previous couple of years—was it time to let all that go? Or pull in the reins?

To be honest, he wasn't sure which.

"Feels like things are moving fast." He stood and took a couple of steps toward his dad's bookshelves, glancing over his collection of ranching books and western novels. *Are we moving in the right direction, Dad?*

Ethan stood, too. "I think we're still just brainstorming here. Nothing written in stone yet."

"Are we moving too quickly for you, Evan?" He could feel Jessica's stare.

Turning, he said, "I value your opinion. You know the facts surrounding the financial health of this ranch better than any of us, and you know the markets. I would like to hear your take on it. Figure out if this bison venture is really our best way forward before we make any concrete plans."

"We need information before we can plan, Evan," Brandley said. "All I want from Nate is information."

"Of course." He looked out the window. Why were his insides suddenly rioting with doubt?

Jessica rose and grasped his elbow. "Take a walk with me." She turned to Ethan and Brandley. "Do you mind if I steal him away for a few minutes?"

* * *

Time to get the cowboy out of the past and think toward the future.

Whether a do-or-die moment, or not, she wasn't certain, but Jessica felt an enormous need to set some things straight—in her mind, at least, if not in Evan's.

"Not at all," Brandley said. "Nolan is fussy and needs a nap. I'll get him down. When you come back, if you need anything at all, the office is open to you."

Smiling, Jessica nodded. "Thanks, Brandley. You've been more than helpful."

Ethan headed for the door. "I'm going to get the crew started on cleaning and fixing that baler. I'll check in with everyone later this morning." He glanced at Evan. "You know, whatever you decide is fine with me."

Evan nodded. "I do."

Jessica took a moment to gather her thoughts as Ethan and Brandley left. While touched by Evan's sincerity, and perhaps a subtle admission of doubt, she also knew his query was normal. What he'd controlled for so long was quickly slipping through his fingers.

"Jessica, look—"

She interrupted him, wanting to put some space in the conversation. "Cute couple." She nodded toward the door Ethan and Brandley had just exited.

Evan stepped closer, looking a little puzzled. "They've had their rough patches but have worked through them."

"Married long?" she asked.

"About a year. Well, and a couple of years right after high school."

"Oh?" She looked up into Evan's eyes. Goodness, he seemed taller. Maybe her heels weren't as high.

He grinned. "Long story. They married young. Ethan went into the Navy and then into SEAL training. They divorced and were separated for years until Ethan came home injured."

"That's terrible. The PTSD, right?"

"And some physical injuries, too. That took a while to heal."

"Is he okay now?"

Ethan exhaled. "He has his days but is so much better now that Brandley is back in his life. His leg will never be the same and he still suffers from PTSD. All said, he's good, and we're glad he's back home."

Jessica thought about that. "So, while he was gone, you managed the ranch?"

"I did. With Dad, of course, but he was slowing down."

"And that's why you feel so determined to make this work?"

"That's why I have to find a solution. I feel like I let people down."

Ah. There it is.

It was important that she figured out the root cause of Evan's mistrust. While confident it wasn't directed at her, and more so at the bank, she wasn't entirely certain.

Regardless, her approach to the dilemma should come from a pragmatic viewpoint—by the numbers, no emotion involved. That's what an impartial banker would do, particularly one told to resolve the issues satisfactorily for the family, the bank, and the community.

And the bank signed her paychecks, so that meant she had to do the best job possible for them. But would they even consider the bison proposal?

But how does what's best for the bank affect the ranch? For Evan and his family? Particularly if he feels like he is letting the family down?

"I don't want you to feel that way, Evan."

"Some things are simply difficult to let go of."

"I'm sure. Let's get some fresh air."

Evan led her out of the office, through the great room, and out the side door facing the barn. "Let's walk out toward the south pasture. Less cow patties there right now." He grinned.

"Good thought. I have these shoes to consider."

"There is that."

She paused for a few seconds. "Except... Hold on."

Hurrying toward her SUV, she opened the passenger side door, pulled out a pair of boots, and sat for a moment, changing her heels for cowgirl boots. She'd bought them just the other day, and hadn't even broken them in yet, but no time like the present.

Looking up, she caught Evan's sexy, sideways grin. Her cheeks warmed.

"I like those," he said. "Ariat?"

"Yes, sir." She stood, closed the truck door, and walked past him. "Let's take that walk now."

They took the path behind the house and down the fence row of the pasture.

"There are definite advantages to partnering with Nate," she began. "Bison are heartier than cattle, more suited to the climate here. And their meat commands higher prices." She paused for a moment, looking out past the barns. "We need to check on the stability of the market, though. The economy is rather high right now, so people can afford the luxury of more expensive food products, but if the economy tanks, will the customer base remain?"

"Can we do some market research?"

"I think we should. I can do that for you."

He met her gaze. "That would be great."

Jessica's heart did a little dance.

She turned away, breaking their eye contact, and watched a hawk circling lazily overhead. "The addition of a bison herd to Sweet Grass would mean major changes for your operation. New grazing patterns, different equipment." Jessica glanced at Evan. "And if prices fell, you could be vulnerable. All your eggs in one basket, so to speak. Were you planning to keep a cattle herd, too?"

Evan nodded, hands in his pockets. "Yes. A smaller herd, I think. Don't you?"

"I do."

"What about Gage's offer?" he asked.

Jessica frowned. She didn't know Gage Parker but had conducted a little research online. He owned a mega-hotel conglomerate which spanned North America and was currently buying several ranches in Montana and surrounding states. She worried his land purchases were for potential hotel sites or destination resorts—but didn't want to alarm Evan about all that until she knew more. There was nothing to show that in her research—it was simply a gut hunch, but her gut rarely steered her wrong.

"I can get behind selling the cabin and the surrounding acreage, as I told your mother, but I'm hesitant about selling the entire ranch. I think that's a little extreme at this point."

Evan's shoulders seemed to relax. "Good. I've been worried about that. I think my brothers feel the same."

"Selling out might help in the short-term," she said carefully. "But what then? Where would you live? How would you all earn a living? Have you thought about that?"

Evan halted and stared at the ground. "No. I haven't. That damned near made my heart stop when you said the words."

She moved closer. "Then let's not go there."

He lifted his gaze. "I don't think selling out to Gage is the best plan. My soul couldn't take it."

"I understand that more than you know."

"You do, don't you?"

Her gaze dropped from Evan's eyes to his lips. She wanted him to kiss her again, wanted him to sweep her into his arms and hold her tight until it was all said and done—but this was not the time.

Would there ever be a right time? She didn't know.

Stumbling back a half step, she turned and began walking again. "My recommendation would be to partner with Nate. It's higher risk, but with that risk comes greater potential reward." Jessica turned again and caught his gaze. "And it means you keep control of your ranch's future."

Evan looked thoughtful, turning over her words. She'd cut right to the heart of both offers, clarifying the stakes and trade-offs. She hoped her insight would prove valuable as he weighed this critical decision for his family's future.

"I appreciate your candor," he said finally. "Giving me a lot to think on."

Jessica grinned, hoping she had helped give clarity.

"You know, last night, my mom told me to decide—with Ethan and Dylan, of course, and then let the rest of them know. I think I know what we should do."

"And that is?"

His gaze pierced hers. "We should get the cabin and two-hundred acres on the market and take the highest offer, whether it's Gage or someone else. Then if all your research goes well, and we get the bank approval, we partner with Nate."

Jessica's heartbeat kicked up a notch. "I think that's an excellent plan."

"We still have work to do, right?"

"Yes. Getting our ducks in a row to present this to the powers-that-be at the bank."

"Then let's do it. Since you're here, maybe we could go over some of these numbers again. I could call Nate and get him to come by, instead of Brandley going to him. Maybe we could get a lot of this ironed out by this afternoon."

Jessica nodded, rolling up her jacket sleeves. "Let's take another look at those books. And yes, call Nate."

* * *

For the next few hours, they pored over financial statements, profit-and-loss reports, and balance sheets. A level of ease developed between them as they worked. Evan appreciated Jessica's thoughtful analysis and the way she asked considerate questions. He found her willingness to listen and consider different perspectives refreshing.

"You should run this place," Evan joked during a lull. "Seems like you've got a better handle on the money side of things than any of us."

"Oh, I don't agree. Brandley has done an excellent job, Evan."

He certainly knew that. "I didn't mean to imply she wasn't. The thing is, she is so busy with the baby now and working outside of the ranch to make extra income. She has little time to focus here."

"Do you need to hire a new bookkeeper?"

"I could never do that to her."

"She might welcome the help, Ethan."

He eyed her, wondering... "You couldn't...could you?"

Jessica laughed and shook her head. "Well, maybe when I tire of the banking world. Honestly, it would be a conflict of interest. Maybe I could recommend someone if we get to that point."

Their eyes met and held for a moment.

Evan cleared his throat and shuffled the papers into a neat stack. "I think going through all of this gives me clarity," he said. "Your help is invaluable, Jessica. I don't know how to thank you."

"Just doing my job," she replied.

A knock sounded at the door, and Ethan popped his head into the office. "Brandley wanted me to tell you she can't join you. Nolan is sick, and she's taking him to Rapid to the clinic."

"Oh, no..." Jessica said. "I'm so sorry to hear that."

Evan took in Jessica's sympathetic expression. She was genuinely concerned.

"Thanks, Jessica." Ethan glanced at his brother. "I'm heading back out to the barn."

"Wait, if you have a minute."

"Sure."

Evan paused, looking out the window, and then back to his brother. "We've been reviewing the statements and the previous five-year plan, and weighed the pros and cons of the current proposals. There's more research to do, but Ethan, I'm leaning toward not selling the ranch to Gage—maybe just the cabin and acreage—and exploring the proposal with Nate. Jessica thinks it could work."

Jessica rose beside him. "I still have to get the plan together and present to the board."

"And we need to talk to Nate. He is dropping by later."

Ethan took a deep breath. "I'm with you all the way. Please understand, I'm not trying to push this off on your shoulders alone. I trust you, Evan. You ran this place for a long time and know it better than anyone. I'm behind you one hundred percent."

It wasn't often that Evan experienced the burn of tears, but at that moment, he did. "Thank—"

He didn't get the words out before Ethan caught him up in a bear hug. "Thank you," he whispered.

Evan leaned back, holding Ethan's gaze for a few seconds longer.

"I should get going." Jessica gathered her things, sliding the folders into a leather bag. "Let me know if you need anything else."

"Wait. Don't rush off just yet. Nate may still come by." He wasn't ready for her to leave. "Stay a little longer?"

She stared down at her cell phone and hesitated a moment before responding, then hooked her gaze with his. "It's almost lunchtime and I should get back to the office. They frown on us being out of the office for too long. Besides, I have to prepare the plan for the board committee. You know what we want to discuss with Nate. Call me at the office if you have questions."

"Alright."

She lifted her bag to her shoulder and smiled at Ethan, then Evan. "I'm off."

Chapter Ten

Jessica's gaze fell on the spreadsheets and documents laid out across her kitchen table. Her afternoon had not gone as planned, so she'd slipped the most important Sweet Grass files into her briefcase and brought the work home for the weekend.

Mr. Nelson had called a meeting with her and her immediate supervisor, Charles Short, as soon as she'd returned to the office, taking up a good ninety minutes of her afternoon. It seemed unlikely the man called such intensive meetings off the cuff, unless something was urgent. She knew his schedule was full because it had taken her several days to book a meeting for her initial orientation.

Ever since their afternoon discussion, she'd felt uneasy. Rubbing her temples, she recalled the conversation.

"I understand there is a legitimate offer to buy Sweet Grass Ranch, Ms. Chase. What can you tell me?"

She was surprised that Mr. Nelson had somehow gotten wind of Gage Parker's offer, and it soon became clear he would not disclose how. Had Gage contacted him? Who else would do that?

"There is an informal offer on the table," she told him. "But it was very casual, more of an opening conversation. They discussed no price, and the family is uncertain whether it is the right way to go. We do have a plan to sell Mrs. MacKay's cabin and two-hundred surrounding acres and will move forward with that sale soon."

He shook his head. "No. That's just another stop-gap attempt. Look into the full sale."

Jessica felt herself physically jerk at his abrupt words.

While she and Mr. Short cautioned against such a bold move, Nelson insisted she begin discussions with the family and negotiate a deal with Gage Parker.

"But isn't that putting the cart before the horse?" she said. "We've not taken the necessary steps to force a sale. We aren't there yet, Mr. Nelson. Besides, I've been focusing my efforts in the opposite direction."

"Then refocus." He glared across the desk, his gaze intense.

"But, sir."

"Move things along, Ms. Chase. There are steps to take here, and we don't make these kinds of decisions lightly," Mr. Nelson had told her. "I've spoken with the board committee, so work with Chuck to make sure we don't misstep."

She'd looked at him, making direct eye contact, and shared her position. "With all due respect, sir, I feel this isn't the right move. I've been creating a plan with their accountant and the family and—"

He interrupted. "Their accountant has been making and executing plans for a couple of years now. It's not working."

Jessica waited a full two seconds before speaking. An attempt to hold her rising concern. "Again, with respect, this is a workable plan, with much potential. Also, a neighboring rancher has put forth another idea, and I think we should explore that."

His left brow shot up. "Another offer to buy? That's good news. We could have a bidding war."

"Oh, no." Jessica scooted to the edge of her seat, leaning closer. "A business proposition, with Nate Brave Eagle, who wants to expand his bison operation, initially leasing grazing land, with the potential for a future business partnership."

Lance Nelson jolted forward in his seat and belly laughed. Leaning closer, his smile disappearing, he said, "Miss Chase, not one buffalo will step foot on Sweet Grass Ranch. Mark my word. Now, you have work to do."

With a wave of his hand, she and her supervisor were dismissed.

After that meeting, she'd been chastised again by Mr. Short, for bucking up against Lance Nelson—which apparently, was never done. "I'd like your plan for the sale of Sweet Grass Ranch on my desk by two o'clock Monday afternoon."

Impossible. How could she do that? In her heart, she knew there was a better way.

She had the weekend to figure it out.

Blowing out a breath, she looked over the paperwork, a queasy feeling settling in her stomach. She might lose her job, but she had to do what was right. Hopefully, it wouldn't come to that.

She'd reviewed her notes from her call with Nate and Brandley earlier, analyzing the financial details and long-term viability of each option. At the time, she was confident in her assessment. The bison partnership offered obvious benefits and was the wiser choice for the ranch's future.

She was certain of it, no matter what Lance Nelson thought.

But looking at the pages of calculations and projections, doubt crept in.

Was her past clouding her judgment? She left her dream of ranch life behind when she was in high school. That was another lifetime ago. Was she subconsciously trying to save the family ranch—her family ranch—that no one could save when she was a kid?

Was selling out to Gage actually better for the MacKay family in the long run?

She picked up the phone and called Evan, not entirely certain she knew what she would say, but felt the need to connect.

"Hello?"

"Hi, Evan. It's Jessica. I'm sorry it's late. Do you have a minute?"

"Sure. Everything okay?" he asked.

Jessica sighed. "Yes, I think. I'm just second guessing myself. What if I'm steering you wrong?"

"Why would you think that?"

"Because of my personal history."

A few seconds of silence passed. "Tell me more about that?"

Jessica hesitated. "There are things from my childhood... I fear they may be clouding my judgement. I want what's best for you and the ranch."

Evan didn't immediately respond. "Do you want to tell me what worries you?"

Not tonight. No. "Another time. Okay?"

"Alright. I trust you, Jessica. Your insight, your expertise. That's what I need. The past is the past. Let's let it stay there."

She would if she could.

But somehow, the last of her reservations melted away just by talking with him. A part of her wanted to allow the growing connection between them to blossom. But now was definitely not the time for her to explore a cowboy crush. "It's getting late. I should let you go."

"Jessica...."

"We can discuss the proposals more next week," she said briskly. "Goodnight, Evan."

"Wait. Just a minute. Wait please."

She held onto the phone. "I'm still here."

"Tomorrow is Saturday. You don't have to work, do you?"

"No. Not really. I mean, I brought work home, but that's flexible."

"Then meet me at the ranch, say two o'clock tomorrow afternoon? Time to break in those boots of yours—and dress warmly. As cute as you looked today in your suit and cowboy boots, I think jeans may be more appropriate."

"What in the world, Evan?"

"Just come. See you at two."

He clicked off, and Jessica set her phone aside. She wished she could set her worries aside as easily.

* * *

"Remember when we were kids and raced to get the horses ready?" Evan grinned at the memory, glancing over at Ethan.

He stood in the dusty barn, running his hand along the flanks of his buckskin, and the worn leather of the saddle he'd had for years. The familiar scents of hay and horses brought him back to his childhood, when he and Ethan would scramble to be the first one to saddle up.

Ethan chuckled, leaning against the stall door. "Yeah, and you always won because you shoved me out of the way."

"That's not how I remember it," Evan shot back with a grin.

They had led most of the horses out to the corral for the day. His smile faded as he glanced around the empty barn. Decades of memories etched into every beam and board.

"Do you ever think about the next MacKay generation,

Ethan? Will our kids run this ranch? Or does the legacy die with us?"

Ethan laid a hand on his shoulder. "I have a feeling our kids are going to be here doing the same things we're doing."

Evan took comfort in his brother's reassurance.

"By the way," Ethan added, "Have you talked with Mom yet about your discussion with Jessica yesterday? About the potential partnership with Nate?"

He shook his head. "Not yet. I want to give it the weekend to mull things over in my head. I'm not ready for Mom's questions yet."

"I get that. Where are you off to this afternoon?"

"Just for a ride," he told Ethan.

"Alone?"

Securing the cinch, Evan shrugged. "Why do you ask?"

"You're getting two horses ready."

Evan stepped back, eyeing the mare and gelding. Both were great quarter horses. He figured the chestnut mare would be good for Jessica. His horse, Nomad, was the buckskin. He glanced at Ethan, feigning surprise. "I am? Well, how about that? I like choices."

Ethan rolled his eyes. "You also like that woman sitting in her Tahoe out in the lot."

Evan turned. "Do not."

"Do so."

They both laughed like they were kids again.

"She's already here?" Evan took a step toward the barn door.

"And waiting."

"Well, shit." He made sure both horses were secured to their stall gates and headed out of the barn. As he entered the bright sunshine of the afternoon, he squinted at the endless prairie behind the house, the tall grasses rippling in the breeze. The

Black Hills jutted up from the horizon. Maybe they'd ride toward the hills.

He approached the Tahoe, calling out her name.

Jessica got out of her truck, wearing jeans, a heavy sweater, and her boots.

"Now, that's more like it," he said.

Jessica laughed.

* * *

Minutes earlier, Jessica had checked her watch again and again, wondering if she'd gotten her wires crossed. Normally, when she'd pulled up to the ranch house, Evan greeted her. He'd been cryptic about their plans for the afternoon, so her curiosity was definitely piqued.

Then he appeared from the shadowy depths of the barn.

"Jessica!" His voice broke through her reverie as he approached, his tall, rugged frame casting a long shadow on the ground. She exited the vehicle and met his gaze, which seemed to sparkle as he strode up to her.

"Now, that's more like it," he said, grinning, and looking her over.

Jessica glanced down at herself. "Definitely not a work outfit."

"I like it."

She grinned.

"Glad you could make it. I've got a surprise for you."

"Oh?" That mysterious glint in his eyes intrigued her. "What is it?"

He extended his hand. "Follow me."

Jessica's heart swelled a little at the strength of his grip, the callouses on his hands—evidence of a man who truly knew hard work. "Are you going to tell me what we're doing?"

"Nope, it's a surprise." His eyes twinkled with mischief.

Inside the barn, Evan stopped in front of a beautiful, well-groomed chestnut mare. "This is Daisy. I picked her out for you to ride today." He smiled warmly at Jessica, as if gauging her reaction.

"We're riding?"

"Yes, ma'am. If that's okay with you."

"Very much. I'm excited!" She stroked the horse's velvety muzzle. Daisy nestled her nose in the palm of her hand, and Jessica's heart swelled with affection for the animal. Her stomach clutched with the nostalgia of home in Wyoming. It had been a long time since she'd been around horses. The mare was a beauty.

She turned and studied Evan. "This is quite a surprise. And to be honest, a gift."

He gave her a slight smile. "I'm glad you like the idea."

"I do."

Evan stepped closer to the mare, rubbing her nose. "I wanted you to see more of the ranch. It's best seen on horseback."

Jessica hesitated, her eyes darting between Evan and Daisy. Her heart raced at the thought of spending an afternoon riding with him. There was something vulnerable and earnest in his eyes, as if he were revealing a piece of his soul by inviting her into his world.

"I haven't ridden since..." Her words trailed off, memories of her childhood flooding back. *Hope I still remember how. Nonsense. Just like riding a bike. Right?*

"We'll take it nice and easy," he said, patting the mare's neck. "This old girl is gentle and follows direction well. No worries. You'll be safe with her if that concerns you."

"No, I'm not concerned." Jessica tilted her head, assessing

the mare. Inwardly, she smiled a little. "She's really lovely, Evan. But I'm just... Wondering about her, um, spirit?"

Evan frowned. "She's as gentle as they come. I figured she'd be good for you."

Jessica ran a hand down the mare's neck and threaded her fingers into the horse's mane. "She's a beautiful girl. I'm sure she is a wonderful ride."

"Like I said, she's gentle and used to women. She's my mom's horse, but she doesn't ride her as much anymore. You'll be fine with her."

Jessica cocked a brow. "Oh, I get it."

"What?"

"You take me for a city slicker." She made eye contact, hoping her stern look and furrowed brow would send a message. She didn't want him to know she was actually teasing. Not yet anyway.

"Well, I assumed...."

"Come on," Jessica sweet-talked, and kicked up one foot. "You think I have these boots for a fashion statement?" She perused the horses again. "I'll ride the buckskin. What's his name?"

"Nomad." Evan laughed. "And he's my horse."

Her lips rolled into a smirk. "Does that mean I can't ride him?"

"Yeah, Evan. Does that mean she can't ride old Nomad?" Grinning, Ethan stepped out of a stall, leading a palomino.

Jessica grinned. "Hi, Ethan."

"Afternoon, ma'am." He dipped his head.

"I don't want you to get hurt," Evan said.

"Bring on the gelding, mister. I can hold my own."

Ethan guffawed.

Evan slanted his head to the side and studied her. "Well, alright then. Give me a minute."

Relenting, he took the palomino's reins from Ethan and saddled the horse.

"I'll give Daisy a quick ride," Ethan said, reaching for the mare's reins. "And then put her up. You two go on."

Evan nodded. He handed the buckskin over to Jessica and led the palomino out of the barn. She followed, and he had to force himself not to look back.

Once outside, Jessica swung herself expertly into her saddle, gathered the reins, and looked down at Evan. Her face ached to smile.

Hoisting himself onto his horse, Evan paused, then cautioned, "Just say the word if you want to switch."

"Alrighty."

Flashing a smile, she nudged the gelding into a canter. Easing into a gallop, she took off up the hill behind the house, wind whipping through her hair as the horse moved gracefully beneath her. The buckskin's hooves struck the earth with confidence. With every thump, his hoofbeats vibrated against the hard soil, radiating into her being. She absorbed the rhythm of the gelding's run and felt his power coursing through her veins.

The breeze in her face held the sweet fragrance of dust and pine. Smiling against the sensations, she breathed in every essence. Every particle.

Smelled like freedom. Felt like home.

She was twelve years old again. Riding the wind.

Chapter Eleven

Evan laughed aloud. The woman kept him guessing, that was for certain.

Jessica effortlessly guided the horse up the hill, riding like she was born in the saddle, completely at ease. When he caught up with her, they slowed the horses and ambled along the ridge side-by-side for a while. They stayed silent, but Evan felt an energy between them that was nearly palpable. Stealing a quick glance or two her way, he wondered if she sensed it, too.

The day was perfect for riding—a cool breeze, the sun not too hot, the day crisp and on the cusp of winter. When they drifted to a stop, they turned their horses to look out over the ranch. Beside him, he heard Jessica sigh. He scanned the countryside, too, as if taking in the rolling grasslands and the infinite blue sky for the first time. The prairie below lay bathed in the fading golden light of afternoon.

"So beautiful up here." Jessica sighed. "I'm in awe."

Evan nodded. "I've always loved it."

"Peaceful."

For a moment, he examined her pretty profile—high cheekbones, plump lips. "I like to come up here in the mornings. Gets my day off to a good start."

Turning, Jessica smiled. "I imagine it would."

She looked back toward the horizon again, the ranch house and barns below. Her breathing became shallower, and her shoulders appeared to relax as she settled into the saddle.

"I have to say that was a bit of a surprise a few minutes ago."

"Oh?"

"You ride well."

She gave him a shy smile. "I hope you know I was teasing you."

"And here I thought you were mad at me."

"No. Never." She paused, her gaze scraping the landscape. "I spent a lot of time on ranches when I was a girl. Did I tell you that?"

"In passing, I think. Wyoming?"

Jessica met his gaze with a thin smile. "Yes. On a couple of ranches near Wheatland. My parents' ranch was smaller, an offshoot of the cattle ranch my grandparents owned. The land was in our family for a couple of generations. Dad would have inherited that ranch, too, if things hadn't gone haywire. Those were good times, though, even if life was hard." She shook her head, as if shaking off the memories.

"I'm sorry. That must've been tough."

She stared off into the distance. "It was. I was very young when we moved. But the land, living on the ranch and being around horses, it was my whole life back then. When Dad had to sell out, it broke my heart. My grandparents' hearts, too. But they understood why it had to happen."

Evan sat silent for a moment, giving her time to settle into her memories. "So that's what you meant last night when you called—that you don't want your childhood to cloud your judgement?"

She nodded. "I don't remember all the details about why we had to sell. I was too young to understand, maybe six or seven years old, but I know it was money related. My parents worried about money. I also remember cattle dying. My mom was sick a lot and there were medical bills, too. Dad finally threw in the towel and sold the place, got a job at a factory in Cheyenne, and we moved."

"I imagine that was hard on everyone."

"Yes." Her gaze skittered off his then, looking over the hills. "The upside was that I got to live with my grandparents on their ranch until I was fourteen."

A smile played over her lips. "The best years of my life, until... Well, until that ranch sold too."

Evan fell silent for a few minutes as she stared ahead. "Do you want to tell me about that?"

She kept staring off in front of her, as if her gaze were falling on distant memories. She took a minute to gather her thoughts, and her words, perhaps, nearly speaking at one point, then pausing again. Evan waited as she wrestled with it all.

"It was a difficult time in my life," she began. "Dad ended up working overtime most days to make ends meet and to pay for his beer money. For a little while, Mom worked two jobs to help. He became a different man, and I was pretty much on my own. I came home from school to an empty house, fixed myself dinner, did my homework, and put myself to bed. There were nights I wasn't even sure he came home."

Evan edged the horse closer to Jessica and reached for her hand. She cautiously let him take it and hold it while she still gazed off.

"I'm sorry, Jessica."

She sniffled and glanced down. "Thanks. It's okay. I suppose in some ways all that strengthened me for what was to come."

"Oh?"

"That's when I stayed summers with my grandparents. Mom and Dad didn't know what to do with me once school was out. But I loved it so much and was happy at Western Hills." Her voice lowered, became softer. "I loved them both so much...."

"Western Hills?"

"Oh, that was the name of my grandparents' ranch back then. I'm sure it's changed now." She blinked away the nostalgia and turned to Evan, her eyes glistening. Abruptly changing the subject, she said, "I want Sweet Grass to thrive, Evan. This ranch is special. Like the ones I knew growing up. I don't want you to lose your family home."

Something shifted between them. Her words resonated deeply, assuring him she understood what made Sweet Grass so precious—perhaps because of what she'd experienced personally. He was truly touched that she felt so deeply, and truly cared about him and his family, and their ranch.

"Jessica, I'm sorry about your family."

She jerked a quick nod and lifted her gaze, making eye contact. "I don't want to talk about it anymore right now."

"Okay." He reached out and cupped her cheek, tenderly caressing with his thumb. "You don't have to say another word." She pressed into his hand and closed her eyes.

Evan savored the moment. After a while, he tried to shift the mood a little too, and lowered his hand. "I'm glad you are working with us on behalf of the bank. I feel better with you on our side."

Jessica smiled softly. "I'm happy to help you."

He fell silent for a minute. "I do owe you an apology."

"What?" Her brow furrowed. "Oh? No, you don't."

"I do. I was wrong about you. I made a lot of assumptions.

Now I realize all you want is to help. I hope you can forgive me."

She placed her hand over his. "Nothing to be sorry about, but if it makes you feel better, then I accept your apology."

He smiled and turned her hand over, squeezing it. "Thank you."

"You're welcome."

She shifted in her saddle then, as if dismissing that conversation, and pulled her hand away. They both took up their reins while their horses pranced a little. Her gaze played over the ranch below. "That's your mom's cabin over there. Right? It looks different from this vantage point."

"It is."

"And is this the acreage that would sell?"

"Yes." He pointed. "I'm thinking we'd survey off from that hill over there, all the way over to that stand of trees on our left."

Jessica sighed. "That has to be some of the prettiest parts of the ranch." She watched Evan's face as he stared out over the hills.

"It is. I hate to see it go."

"I wish it didn't have to."

"Well, that's a discussion for another day," he interjected, eager to get off that subject. "Come on, let's head over this way."

Evan nudged his horse and Jessica followed. They ambled farther along the ridge in silence for several minutes. After a while, Ethan slowed, allowing Jessica to pull up beside him. "Tell you something?"

Jessica turned. "Of course."

"I am concerned about the future," he began. "I know we have options and that you are working on things, but if the bank calls in our loan, I don't know how we'll make it. I honestly don't know how I will make a living."

Jessica listened intently, letting him continue, her face etched with concern.

"I suppose Ethan and Brandley will be fine. They can survive on Ethan's military benefits and Brandley's work. The younger twins—they need an attitude adjustment anyway, so maybe it could be good for them. Dylan has always worked off the ranch. Me? This place has been my entire life. I don't know that I'm good at anything else... And apparently, I'm not very good at this."

"Evan. That's not true." Her eyes were full of concern. "Maybe let's not put the cart before the horse?"

He met her gaze. "I know you have to do your job. I'm not expecting any favors. None of us are. But I'm asking you to consider what this place represents. Not just to me, but to the family, and frankly, this entire community."

"I understand. Truly, I do."

"And I also want you to know that if selling this section of land saves the rest, we are all good with it."

Jessica searched his eyes and leaned closer. He could sense the sincerity in her expression. "I promise you, Evan, that I'm taking everything into account."

He was grateful she was willing to listen. "Thanks for letting me get that off my chest. I know you are doing your best to save this ranch for our family."

Jessica's expression froze for a second. She half-nodded, then shook her head, as if shaking the uncertainty away. "I only hope I can succeed. There are a lot of things to consider, and sometimes that is not always a good thing."

He met her gaze and held it. "I trust you, Jessica."

She gave a slight nod, then tugged on her horse's reins. "Heading down?"

"Yup."

As they turned their horses toward the cabin, Evan felt

something jerk in his gut. The anxious look on her face was difficult to ignore.

* * *

Maybe you shouldn't trust me. Maybe I should just tell you the truth.

The words were on the tip of her tongue. Thank goodness she didn't let them fly. There was time enough to tell him and the family the news about the bank—but it was her hope she could turn things around by Monday afternoon, so they never had to know how close they'd come to losing the ranch.

She had to save Sweet Grass Ranch. Had to.

When this is all said and done, Evan MacKay, I hope you can forgive me.

A thud of regret landed in her tummy. Nudging the buckskin forward, she followed Evan as the horses picked their way down a rocky part of the hill.

"Mind if we stop in for a quick visit at the cabin with Mom and Noah?" Evan called over his shoulder. "Maybe we can share more about the plan with Nate."

Jessica tried to push her uncertain thoughts away. "Of course. It would be great to see your mom again."

Ethan smiled, and suddenly her heart felt a little lighter. What with her discussion of her family and the past, and her knowledge of how the bank felt about Sweet Grass Ranch, she'd grown a little melancholy.

She fell silent as they navigated down the hill, immersed in her own wandering thoughts. Her rehashing of the past, and Evan's words had stirred up emotions long buried.

She pictured her father's weathered hands guiding her own as he taught her how to ride. She remembered her mother's voice singing old cowboy songs as she made dinner. The pungent scent of hay and horses enveloped her once again.

Jessica blinked back tears as she realized just how much she had missed that life. The open skies, the hard work, the connection to the land—it all had meant everything to her family, too. It's what represented home and family to her—always had. And suddenly, she missed it all so very much.

Cold corporate boardrooms and endless paperwork filled her days. While her career had brought prestige and financial success, it lacked the fulfillment her ranch roots had provided.

She had a tough road ahead. Weighing the bank's priorities against the needs of the MacKay family would take her experience in that corporate world, and also her sentiment toward the situation—and probably some old-fashioned grit and gut instinct. But deep in her heart, she knew she could not ignore the pull of her past. The way of life still called to her, reminding her of who she was and where she came from. Evan had helped her reconnect to that truth.

Whatever happened, she was at a turning point. She'd been right to leave Cleveland behind and head west. She just had to figure out where home was.

For a moment, she contemplated that sense of freedom again. Then she took a deep breath, releasing the memories, and turned her gaze firmly ahead. Back to the future, and the decisions that lay before her.

"Well, here we are."

Jessica savored the last rays of sun on her face as she dismounted her horse. Evan slid off his horse too, then took the buckskin's reins, leading both horses toward the corral, and securing them to the fence.

Jessica noticed a pickup truck parked beside the porch. A back door was open on the extended cab, and suitcases lay on the back seat.

Connie bustled out of the house. "My goodness! Come in, you two. How about something to drink?"

Evan stepped closer. "That would be great, Mom. I'm parched." He turned to Jessica. "You?"

"Absolutely."

She moved forward and Evan put his hand on her back as they approached the porch and a smiling Connie. She motioned them inside. "We are getting ready to leave, you know. Sarah is in a tizzy and needs some help."

She rushed toward the refrigerator and pulled out a pitcher of iced tea, pouring a glass for each, setting them on the kitchen island.

Evan motioned to a stool and Jessica sat. He did the same.

"You're leaving when?" he asked his mother.

She glanced at her watch. "In about...."

"You ready, Connie, honey?" Noah moved into the room, stopping up short. "Oh, didn't realize we had company."

"We dropped in unexpectedly. Don't want to hold you up," Evan said.

"Nonsense. Drink your tea." Connie hurried off to grab her purse from a chair in the great room. Then she moved back to give him a hug. "I'll call you. Sarah is fretting because she has to go back to work, some event in Denver, and she doesn't want to leave the baby. Now, Cole is perfectly capable, of course, but she's a new mother and all, and well, she needs me. I don't know how long...."

Her words faded as she slid her gaze over to look at Jessica.

"And my dear, I know you are working hard on this ranch dilemma. Please keep me informed. Will you?"

"Of course, Mrs. MacKay."

"Parker," she reminded. "But please call me Connie."

"Alright. Connie."

"Good." His mother stepped back, looked the two of them over, then grinned. She turned to Noah. "Let's go."

Evan bolted up off the stool. "Mom. Now? Wait."

She waved him off, walking away and talking over her shoulder. "We need to get going before it gets too late. Love you!"

Then, as if forgetting something, she stopped abruptly, whipped around, and glared at the two of them.

"Son, make Jessica a nice dinner tonight? Won't you? Anything in that refrigerator is fair game, so have at it. In fact, I thawed some beef tips out earlier so those need to be used up. Lord knows it will go bad before we get back here. I had planned to drop them off to Brandley on our way out. Oh, and the cabin will be empty tonight, so...."

Her words dangling, Connie beamed and turned back to Noah, hooked her arm in his, and left the house.

Jessica felt her eyes widen at her exit. She was half afraid to look at Evan.

What his mother had implied was abundantly clear.

Chapter Twelve

"**W**hat just happened here?"

Evan glanced at Jessica, took a few steps toward the back door, pushed the curtain aside with a forefinger, and watched his mother and Noah drive away. "And...they're gone."

"In a flash."

"Yeah."

"Wow."

"Interesting, huh?" He turned and gave Jessica a grin.

"An interesting whirlwind. Is she always like that? When she came to the bank, she was so businesslike."

Evan sighed. He joined Jessica at the kitchen island. "Sarah is her baby, her only girl, and this new grandbaby has her beside herself. She was eager to get going, I guess."

Suddenly, his mother's words rang in his ear. *The cabin will be empty, so....*

Hell, did Jessica pick up on that too? "But it's not a bad idea, you know."

Jessica gave him a blank look. "What?"

"Dinner. Are you hungry?"

Her head bobbed back and forth, in neither a yes nor no response. "Somewhat. But actually, I should probably leave and let you get on with the rest of your day." She glanced out the kitchen window, catching sight of the barn and corral. "We still have the horses to take care of."

Evan took a step closer to Jessica, cupping her elbow in his palm. Touching her, even ever so slightly, sent a warmth through him that was both foreign and welcome. Did she feel the same?

"How about this?" He looked down into her eyes. "I'll take care of the horses, put them up for the night in mom's barn, and you can relax while I do that. Then I'll come back and fix dinner."

Looking up, Jessica took a half-step closer, her gaze dancing over his face. Their bodies aligned and so close, the chemistry between them was palpable.

"How about this?" she breathed. "I'll help you with the horses and then we can both fix dinner. Together." One corner of her mouth turned up. "I'm sort of an equal work, equal pay kind of girl. Besides, I enjoy taking care of horses."

Evan chuckled. "That could work."

Jessica tilted her head. "Um hmm."

Are you flirting with me, Ms. Chase?

His body bent involuntarily toward her, both hands resting on her hips. He wanted to tug her closer, just shy of cave man style, but restrained himself. The pull was too strong for him to ignore, her attraction so anticipatingly sweet, he didn't want to mess with the moment. His mouth hovered a scant inch from hers, aching to capture her lips in a soft caress. His eyes flickered closed and—

She stepped out of his arms, leaving him with nothing but her saucy grin. "Those horses are waiting, cowboy."

Evan exhaled, forcing the tension out of his chest. *Definitely flirting.* "That they are."

"I always loved brushing down my horse after a ride."

"It's part of the experience, I think."

"Yes." Reaching for his hand, she waited, smiling, until he placed his in hers. Grasping his fingers tight, she tugged. "Come on. Let's go do cowboy things. And then maybe, later, I might let you kiss me again."

Grinning like a stupid Cheshire cat, Evan obediently followed Jessica out of the house and across the parking area toward the barn. Occasionally, she'd glance his way, a teasing grin on her face.

An hour or so later, the horses brushed, watered, fed, and put up in Connie's barn, they headed back to the house. Despite Jessica's protests, Evan insisted on preparing dinner himself. He set out to make a quick stew, chopping vegetables and searing the beef tips while he chatted with her.

"Your mom has a nice wine collection," Jessica said. She pulled a bottle from the rack on the counter and met his gaze. "Shall we?"

"Definitely. You pick. There is a corkscrew in the drawer there." He pointed to her left.

"I can handle that."

"Choose a red if you would. I'll add some of it to the stew."

"Yummy."

Jessica uncorked the bottle of red wine, poured two glasses half full, then handed him the bottle. They sipped while Evan finished assembling the stew and set it to simmer.

"I noticed there was a bag of salad mix and some other vegetables in the refrigerator," she told him. "How about I make a salad?"

"That would be great. I saw some frozen rolls in the freezer, so I'll get those in the oven to bake."

Pulling out vegetables and setting them on the counter, Jessica smiled. "Teamwork."

"We make a good team," he commented.

Jessica paused, looking at her assemblage of vegetables. He thought he could see a slight smile easing over her face.

Evan grinned to himself.

They chatted and finished the dinner preparations while the stew simmered. After a while, they settled in at the rustic wooden table in the great room. A simple yet elegant centerpiece of wildflowers graced the center. Evan lit a pair of candles.

"For ambiance," he said, flicking her a smile.

"What? Wine in our stew and now candles? You are a worldly cowboy, Evan MacKay." She took a sip of wine and peered over her glass.

"Well, what can I say? A little bit of social graces can go a long way to soften a prickly cowboy."

"Grumpy cowboy."

"That, too."

Jessica laughed and fingered a petal on the flowers. "These are lovely."

"That's mom's doing," Ethan said. "She owned a flower shop for a while and loved making floral arrangements."

"She's a talented woman."

Evan nodded and handed Jessica a basket of rolls. "She worked hard. I'm glad she's enjoying her retirement and, frankly, I'm happy she has Noah. He was a surprise for all of us, but he's good for her."

Jessica took a bite of stew. "Oh, my goodness, Evan! This stew is fabulous. You are quite the chef to pull off something this flavorful in such a short time."

His grin nearly stretched his face. He could get used to having her around.

Their conversation flowed effortlessly while Evan kept their wine glasses full.

"Tell me about growing up here," Jessica said several minutes later. "I'm sure it wasn't always a struggle."

"Mostly good times, to be honest." Evan glanced off for a moment, melancholy catching hold of him. "There were tough times, of course. But those moments made us stronger and more appreciative of what we had—each other and home." He paused, thinking.

"The worst time was when Dad died. We were all at loose ends then, trying to figure out exactly what was going on with the ranch, and how we were going to move forward."

"I'm sure that was difficult."

"His death was terrible, of course. A drunk driver broadsided him. He died at the scene. Mom lost herself there for a while. Ethan came home on leave but was so stoic and hardened by military life, he couldn't lend much support emotionally. Plus, he was here and gone in the blink of an eye, it seemed. Sarah was busy taking care of Mom and trying not to fall apart herself. Dylan was the rock through it all, but I wonder if he's truly grieved. I wonder that about myself, sometimes, too. And the younger boys—well, they pretty much just rode bulls and roped calves every night they could, physically working out the hurt and anger of losing Dad."

"I know that was rough."

"It's been like that since the day he died, going on three years now." Pausing, he wasn't sure he wanted to talk much more about it.

She waited.

"I don't want to leave the impression that we've always been a bunch of inadequate sad sacks around here. Before Dad died, this ranch was the only place most of us wanted to be. It was a thriving, profitable business. We grew up with dirt on our knees, good physical work, and caring for our animals. The house was full of laughter and joking around, never a dull moment. We boys played sports and rode rodeo. Sarah was a barrel racer and a singer. We flourished as kids growing up here."

On impulse, he reached for her hand and held it. "I had hoped my kids would grow up the same. Safe and secure. Happy."

"You want kids one day?" Her gaze held the hint of unexpected question.

"I do. You?"

She looked away for a moment, then back. "Until recently, I didn't think so, but now I do. I want a family again. I just hope I didn't wait too long."

He squeezed her hand. "You're still a spring chicken."

Laughing, she squeezed back. "Hardly, but thanks."

"I have faith that can still happen for you. If that's what you want."

Her gaze held his. "I hope that for you too, Evan," she whispered.

A flash of worry, or perhaps apprehension, flitted over Jessica's face. Their gazes tangoed for several seconds longer, then Evan released her hand.

"Tell me about your family. I want to know more about you."

* * *

Jessica's heart slammed against her chest at the intimate turn of conversation, the sincere look in Evan's eyes—him sharing his family story, asking her to share hers. She'd grown increasingly torn throughout the evening, wrestling with her growing feelings for him, trying to maintain that professional and personal balance, and ignoring the guilt of keeping the bank's demand a secret.

She hesitated, her pulse racing as she contemplated how much to reveal. She'd embarked down that road a while ago—but not fully. Her story was not one she told often, and she was extremely selective to whom she told it.

But looking into Evan's eyes, seeing the caring and compassion in them she also knew was in his heart, suddenly sharing seemed easy.

She stood, clearing her dishes from the table, and taking them into the kitchen. Staring at the countertop where she placed them, she said, "To be honest, I've always been somewhat guarded with my personal story."

"Just share what you want."

Turning slightly, she noticed Evan stepping up beside her, his dishes in hand. He set them on the counter, then found her hands and peered into her eyes.

Jessica suddenly felt safe.

"I don't want you to be uncomfortable sharing, but just know I care about you, Jessica," he said.

Her heart swelled, as if she could sing her story to its fullest depths, without consequence, to him. "I care about you too, Evan," she said.

He returned a warm smile.

With a sigh, she hesitated for a moment, letting her brain settle on a place to begin. "My grandparents were hardworking people, but so loving and nurturing." Her voice cracked a little with emotion. "They instilled in me the importance of honesty and persistence. They taught me to never give up on my dreams, no matter how difficult the journey."

Evan gripped her hands tighter, his touch offering comfort and understanding. Jessica looked into his eyes, feeling an inexplicable connection to the man whose life had recently become pleasantly entangled with hers.

"They were important to you."

"Yes. Very."

Her chest tightened as she met his gaze, the sincerity in his eyes threatening to undo the defenses she had built so carefully around her. She searched for the right words, her mind racing through memories and emotions she had buried deep long ago.

"I faced some challenges in my younger years," she added, her voice shaky. "I've always felt the need to prove myself, to show that I'm strong enough to handle whatever life throws my way. Sometimes it's difficult to let people in, to trust them with my thoughts and feelings." She faltered, searching his eyes. "But Evan, I trust you."

He gave her a genuine half-smile. "I'm glad you do. And I understand how you feel. I've always been the protector, the one who shoulders the burden for my family and the ranch. But I've come to realize it's okay to lean on others sometimes."

His gentle encouragement gave her the strength to continue.

"Thank you." Taking a deep breath, she felt the weight of her past pressing against her chest. "The work ethic I learned from my grandparents is one reason I am straightforward and maybe a little stubborn in my career. While things are changing, the finance world has traditionally been male oriented, very much so when I started out after college, so I've had to learn to be firm and very guarded in my work—as in my personal life."

He peered deeper into her eyes. "I was hard on you that first day in the office. Made a lot of stupid male assumptions that were likely politically and socially incorrect. I'm sorry I was such a horse's ass."

She chuckled at those words. "No, you are not a horse's ass. I'm rather used to that, as you probably figured, given my comebacks."

His smile broadened. "Maybe we're even then."

"Perhaps." Jessica swallowed hard, feeling the need to move the conversation forward. "Do you remember me telling you about moving to Cheyenne and my dad's problems with alcohol?"

"Yes."

"What I didn't tell you was that not long after we moved to Cheyenne, my mom died." She stopped briefly, closed her eyes, and listened to her own shallow breathing for a moment. Eyes still closed, she continued. "She'd been sick. I didn't know how bad it was. As a kid, I guess you just don't think about what causes your parent to be sick, you just know that she is. Turned out it was cancer. After we left the ranch, she didn't resume treatment. She worked herself to the bone while Dad drank his nights away."

"Oh, sweetheart...."

Jessica blinked her eyes open. "It's okay. I've come to terms with it. But when I came home to find her after school that day.... Well, that's something that sticks with you."

"Oh, Jessica...." He tugged her closer.

While she wanted his closeness, and him holding her was pure bliss, she had to keep going.

"Wait." She placed a hand on his chest. "Let me say the rest before I can't talk anymore."

"Go on, honey." He lifted her chin with a forefinger. "I'm listening."

She nodded. "Dad gave me up. Just gave me away, and I never heard from him again. I have no clue if he is dead or alive. I was only ten years old when I went to live with my grandparents, and those years turned out to be the best four years of my life. But when I was fourteen, they died in a car accident. Their lives snuffed out while I was at school. That's when I went to foster care. It was...difficult."

Evan's gaze softened. "I can't imagine how hard that must have been."

Jessica was grateful for his empathy and support. "It was a trying time, but in ways, it also made me who I am today. I grew resilient and independent. No matter what foster home they shuffled me off to, I put my head down and worked hard at school, got scholarships, and went to college—in Boston and New York, as you saw. And I did it all because one day, I kept telling myself, I was going to buy back my grandparents' ranch."

She sighed, looking away. "Of course, that was a silly, unrealistic little girl's dream."

Slowly, Evan inched his arms around her waist again, pulling her a little closer. "Have you investigated what happened? Do you know who owns it now?"

She exhaled. "No, but frankly, I'll never be able to buy it."

"Dreams do come true, Jessica."

"It takes more than dreams, Evan. That ranch sold twenty years ago, likely for pennies. It's worth a million or two by now." She paused, searching his eyes. "That's why I'm doing everything I can to make sure you do not lose Sweet Grass Ranch."

"But it's not your task alone. I'm in this with you."

Stepping back and out of his embrace, Jessica shook her head. "Yes. But saving your ranch is up to me. The bank expects me to make this right."

"I don't understand."

"Evan, sometimes I build walls around myself to keep everything else at bay." She glanced down at their interlocked fingers, her heart swelling with a mix of fear and hope. "You need to know that. This next week, with the ranch offers and all, I may need to work through all of this on my own, being your liaison to the bank. Of course, I'll consult you and the family, but please trust me."

"I do. But Jessica... You don't have to be so guarded. And

since it's my family ranch, I need to help you. Let's do this together."

She looked up at him, her eyes stinging with unshed tears. "That means more to me than you could ever know. But...."

"But?"

"But the bank expects me to take care of this, and truly, I need to make this work so I can prove myself to them and keep my job."

She'd said too much. "Never mind."

"Please don't sell us out, Jessica. I'm begging you."

"I would never do that. Trust me. Please. My goal is the exact opposite."

A silence fell between them, filled with shared vulnerability. Evan stepped away, creating a little breathing room between them. "No more talk about ranches or banks," he said. "Let's go for a walk. The night is peaceful, and the cool air might help clear our minds."

"Alright." To be honest, she was ready for a change of venue and conversation.

Evan took her hand and led her outside.

Jessica inhaled deeply, the cool air filling her lungs as they strolled along the dirt path behind the cabin. She shivered slightly, and Evan wrapped an arm around her, pulling her close for warmth.

"Sometimes it's good to let go of our burdens, even if just for a minute." His breath felt warm against her ear. "We don't always have to carry them alone."

Jessica leaned into him, comforted by his presence and the gentle understanding in his voice. Not to mention the warmth of his body next to hers and the security of his arms wrapped around her. She could stay like this, forever.

Though she'd kept quiet about the bank's demands, she felt

a sense of relief in sharing her heart with Evan. Were her walls beginning to crumble?

* * *

"I always found comfort in the quiet beauty of a night sky," Ethan said a few minutes later. "It's easy to get lost in thought while surrounded by such tranquility."

He clasped her smaller hand in his as they strolled beyond the barn, the outside security lamps lighting their way. Shadows danced around them, a soft breeze rustling the leaves of a pair of cottonwood trees lining their path. The dusky evening twittered with the soft sounds of crickets and the distant lowing of cattle.

"The city never sleeps. There's always noise, always people... But out here, it's like stepping into another world. A world I didn't realize I missed so much until lately." She stopped and gazed up into the darkening sky. "My goodness, I've not seen stars like this in years."

"Wait until it gets fully dark. They will burst out at you."

Jessica scanned the sky and sighed. "Beautiful."

Evan glanced at her upturned profile. The openness and wonder he saw in her expression tugged at his heart. "Jessica," he whispered, his throat thick with emotion. Slowly, he turned her toward him, almost fearing she would shy away. Quickly leaning in, he pressed his lips to hers.

He hadn't planned that kiss. It was as spontaneous as they come. But it was just as sweet as if he'd anticipated it for weeks. And if he were honest with himself, he had.

As they kissed under the moonlit sky, their lips teasing and tasting, his senses heightened, and his desire escalated. Gathering her closer into his chest, his heart thumping, he deepened the kiss.

When they parted, both breathless, he cupped her face in

his hands and peered deeply into her eyes. "I like you, Jessica Chase," he whispered. "A lot. I don't know how things became like this so quickly, but I'm not arguing with fate, or that you've brought a whole lot of joy into my life, at a time that hadn't previously been so joyous."

"You believe in fate?" she asked softly.

"I believe in this," he responded, leaning in for a second kiss. Was he falling in love with her? He was. Definitely. Suddenly, the thought of a life without her by his side seemed unbearable.

Her breath against his mouth only stirred his passion more, but he held back as she broke away slightly, their lips not more than a whisper apart. "I believe in your kisses," she murmured.

"Can we see where this leads?" he whispered.

She smiled—a slight, knowing smile. "That would be very nice." Leaning in for another kiss, her soft mouth grazed his.

Perhaps sealing the promise they'd both just spoken?

"I should be going," she said after a minute. "Will you take me down to my truck?"

"Reluctantly," he said, grinning. "But before you go," he murmured, pulling her close. Their lips met, a slow dance of emotions swirling around them, each kiss deepening their connection. The world around them seemed to fade away.

"But maybe I have a better idea," he whispered against her lips.

"Oh?"

"Stay with me." *Too soon? Am I out of line? What will she think?*

"Okay," she murmured.

"Really?"

Jessica flashed a tentative but sexy smile. "Yes."

Chapter Thirteen

The next morning, Evan stood on the front porch of the cabin, his cell phone pressed to his ear, listening to Gage Parker prattle on about things he did not want to discuss. Not this morning. The man's call had jerked him out of a warm bed and even warmer arms, so he was not in a particularly good mood.

The morning sun glowed across the ranch, casting everything in a warm golden light, but did nothing to lift the chill settling in his chest.

"It's a solid offer," Gage said firmly in his ear. "More than fair for a place like Sweet Grass Ranch."

"We are not interested in selling the entire ranch. What happened to the offer on the cabin and two-hundred acres?"

"Oh, I definitely want that, too. It's part of the larger package."

"And now you say you want it all? That we give up the ranch house and barns...and what about managing the place, as you mentioned previously? I'm not sure I'm liking how this deal is suddenly changing, Parker."

Gage cleared his throat. "I really think the best plan, Evan,

135

is for you to give up the place one hundred percent. That way you and your family can split the profits, with each of you walking away with a good chunk of change to start over. I don't have the concern of keeping your family busy over the winter and beyond, until I figure out what kind of operation I want to run there."

Evan panicked at his words. "You're not running cattle?"

"I'm not sure yet."

"But what are the alternatives?"

Gage hesitated. "Look, MacKay, that's all down the road. Right now, let me help you and your family get back on your feet."

Evan's frustration with the conversation was making his chest tight. "But we're working on another plan with the bank. With our loan manager. And I'd like to see where that leads us."

A slight pause came from the other end. "Oh?" Gage finally said. "I was not aware of that. According to Lance Nelson, this all needs to be settled soon, and I'm offering you a way out."

Evan stared off over the hills. *You've talked with Nelson? What the hell?* "I'll get back with you."

"I need an answer by Tuesday morning at nine."

Evan swallowed around the lump in his throat. "That's not much time."

"Forty-eight hours, MacKay. Time is money." Gage's tone was serious.

Well, so was he. "We will not be rushed, Mr. Parker."

"Sleep on it. But I expect to hear from you soon."

The line went dead. Evan lowered the phone, gripping it so tightly his knuckles hurt. The number Parker had offered flashed through his mind—more money than he could've dreamed of over a year ago, when the bank had threatened to foreclose. More than enough to pay off debts and for all of them to invest in their futures and turn their lives around.

But money wasn't everything. Not when it came to a legacy like Sweet Grass.

"I'll be damned if you'll take that away, Gage Parker."

Footsteps sounded behind him. Evan turned to see Jessica stepping onto the porch, two mugs of coffee in hand.

"Hi. You're up?"

Grinning, she moved toward him, giving him a quick kiss on the cheek. "I am. Someone didn't wake me."

Standing close to her, his anxiety suddenly ceased. "I like having you in my bed," he whispered, nuzzling her neck.

"Umm, you mean your mother's bed."

Laughing, Evan stepped back. "Now there's a mood killer."

Jessica echoed his chuckle and held out a mug of steaming coffee. "Who was on the phone?"

His worry escalated again. Evan took the coffee, the ceramic cup warm in his palms. "Gage Parker. He made an offer on the entire ranch."

Jessica's dark eyes widened. "What? When did this happen?"

"Just now." Evan took a bracing sip of the hot coffee. "Wants an answer by Tuesday morning."

"Tuesday?" Jessica leaned against the railing beside him. "That's fast."

"Yes, it is." Evan stared out at the land, the rolling grasslands, the creek snaking along the cottonwoods. Sweet Grass was more than dirt and fences. It was his childhood, his heritage. His future children's inheritance. Decades of MacKay blood, sweat, and tears soaked into the soil.

Could he really hand all that over to a stranger?

"I wonder why so quickly?"

"I don't know. Plus, he gave a price he's willing to pay. It's...substantial."

"How substantial?"

His gaze bored into hers. "Let's just say millions."

"Are you tempted?"

"Yes and no." Evan raked a hand through his hair. "I don't know. The money would help. We could start over."

"But?"

Evan met her gaze. "But we wouldn't have Sweet Grass."

Understanding shone in Jessica's eyes. She'd spent enough time there over the past weeks to know what the ranch meant to him.

"We'll figure something out," she said, determination in her voice. "There are other options. We just need time to explore them." She set her coffee mug on the porch railing. "And on that note, I should head back home. I have some work to do this afternoon and I'm sure you have things to discuss with the family. When you are ready, let me know what you are thinking."

"I think I need to mull this over before hitting the family up with this."

"Not a bad idea."

Evan nodded slowly. Jessica was right—perhaps Gage Parker's offer wasn't the only way out of this mess. He wouldn't give up without a fight.

Gage and his money would just have to wait. He wasn't going to be threatened by the billionaire's deadlines.

* * *

Jessica let out a slow breath. She could see the struggle in his eyes as he contemplated Gage's offer. Part of her wished she could make the decision for him, take the burden from his shoulders, but she also knew it was unfair for the MacKays not to be involved. It was their land.

However, Gage Parker had just complicated things.

The bank wanted to be rid of the risk, and the figure Gage offered would be very attractive to the powers-that-be. Convincing Mr. Nelson of the new restructuring wouldn't be easy. She'd have to get creative, find a solution that gave the bank assurances while keeping the ranch solvent. It wouldn't be the first time she found an unlikely answer to a tricky problem.

Jessica placed a hand on Evan's arm, feeling the tension in his muscles. "Hey. We're in this together," she said gently. "Remember? Whatever happens."

Evan covered her hand with his own. His eyes were troubled, but his mouth curved into a hint of a smile.

"I know," he said. "Somehow, we'll figure it out. We have to."

"Let's look at this offer objectively."

Evan's jaw tightened. "You mean you think I should take it?"

"I didn't say that." Jessica kept her voice calm and reasonable. "But twenty million is a lot of money."

"It's not just about money," Evan snapped.

"I realize that. But you have expenses piling up. Loans coming due. How will you cover the payments, let alone invest in the growth you'll need to be profitable?"

Evan whirled to face her. "You think we should sell to that snake? Hand over three generations of MacKay sweat and blood so he can carve it up however he wants?" His eyes blazed.

Taken aback, Jessica said, "First, I don't think Gage Parker is a snake. He is a well-respected businessman. Second, I also don't believe he will carve up the ranch. He believes in preservation."

"And how do you know that?"

"Research. It's my job."

"Well, research what it will take for us to keep the ranch."

She wasn't surprised at his anger, not really, but she couldn't say she liked his attitude or his demeanor at that moment. "What do you think I've been doing the past week? Twiddling my thumbs and hanging around here waiting for you to kiss me?"

His eyes flared. "Well, look where we ended up last night. Maybe you're just looking for a way to get back to ranch living. Is that why you are helping us?"

"Not fair, Evan." That hurt. Her shoulders jerked back, and her guardrails shot back up with them.

"Well, life's not fair."

"You are a horse's ass."

"I thought we established that last night."

She stepped closer. "Look. Let's calm down here before we both say something we regret. I'm just trying to help, Evan. To make sure you look at things from all angles. That's my job."

"Oh, and now I'm a job? Great."

"Evan! You know that's not true."

"Right." He paced the porch, raking a hand through his hair. "Did you know Parker has talked with Lance Nelson already? Were you going to keep that from me?"

"What? No. He's bluffing."

"Oh? You think? I'm not so sure."

"What does that mean?"

He glared. "You know more than you are letting on."

His words stung. Of course, she did. She knew the bank wanted the family to sell, that Gage was gearing up for an offer and for how much, and she hadn't told them that yet because she thought she could be Miss Fixit. Well now, where had that landed her?

"Evan, look. I don't want you to miss out on an opportunity to better the entire family just because you can't think beyond letting go. I don't want you—or your family—to regret turning away millions of dollars because of sentimentality."

"Sentimentality? Oh, and who would buy back her own family ranch if she could? You know you would do that in a heartbeat."

"That's different."

"No, it's not."

He stepped closer. "By the way, are you getting any kind of cut or commission from this Gage Parker deal if it goes through? Will you have enough money then to buy back your Wyoming ranch?"

His words cut deep into her heart, etched against her soul, and she wasn't sure she could forgive him for saying them. "That's unethical and ridiculous. I'm leaving." She twisted away.

"Did that hit a nerve? What have you done, Jessica?"

She whirled back. "I've done nothing but try to help you, Evan. Don't go there. We're talking about you, not me."

"Answer me this, then. How did you know the offer was twenty million dollars? I hadn't told you that."

She swallowed. "You didn't?"

He shook his head. "You knew already, didn't you?"

"Evan, I...."

He bolted toward her. "If you want to help, Ms. Jessica Chase, don't lie to me. Figure out a way to get the bank off my back that doesn't involve selling my family's legacy." Evan brushed past her and stalked down the steps toward the barn. "I need some air. And time. Make that happen."

Jessica watched him go, equally frustrated and heartsick. She wished she could make him understand the realities of his financial situation, but she knew how deep his roots went in the land—and that was playing havoc with his heart and brain.

And she wished she hadn't blurted out that twenty-million-dollar figure. Fact was, Lance Nelson had called her yesterday to tell her that the offer was on the table—and she'd pushed it out of her head and heart not wanting to tell Evan. Yet.

With a heavy sigh, she knew it was time to head back to her apartment. Better to let him cool down and give them both space to think. He'd said he needed time. Right?

Probably not a bad idea.

Besides, she had work to do.

She had to unravel this mess.

* * *

Evan stood at the far end of his mother's barn, hands braced against the weathered railing of the corral, as he gazed out over the ranch. The thought of signing the land over to someone else's control clenched his gut.

Footsteps approached behind him. "I thought you were leaving."

"Not yet."

Evan turned to the sound of his brother's voice. "Ethan. When did you get here?"

"About thirty minutes ago. I guess you didn't see my truck parked at the side of the barn."

"Why'd you come?"

Ethan shrugged. "Well, Brandley insisted. You didn't come home last night. Jessica's truck was still parked at the main house. And the horses were gone. I figured either the wolves got you, or you two were canoodling up here in Mom's cabin."

Evan huffed and looked away. *Canoodling?* There'd been plenty of that. But where was she now? Heading back home, and it was all his damn fault. "That's none of your business."

"Well, sure. Since you're alive, I'll leave you alone." He turned.

"Stop."

Ethan stood in front of him, waiting.

"We need to talk."

"I probably know what about." He stepped to the corral and stood beside Evan. "That was some fight," he said, leaning on the railing beside him. "Jessica's just trying to help, you know."

Evan huffed, hanging his head. "Help herself, more like. All she cares about is making her bank happy."

"Now that's not fair." Ethan bumped his shoulder against Evan's. "And I don't believe that is true. She cares about this place. And about you, although I'm not sure why."

Evan jerked his head up. "Why do you say that?"

"Because you were acting like a full-blown idiot back there a few minutes ago."

"Shit."

"You owe her an apology."

Exhaling hard, Evan pushed away from the fence. "I will. But even if that's true, she wasn't totally honest with me, held some things back. She doesn't understand what the ranch means to us." As soon as he said the words aloud, he felt a little guilty. That wasn't true. Jessica understood what Sweet Grass meant to him.

"Maybe not," Ethan conceded. "But I think otherwise."

He was probably right.

"You are going to have to decide, brother. Which means more to you, the ranch or Jessica? You should think long and hard about that."

Ethan peered out over the land, his expression thoughtful. Evan wasn't sure how to respond. What does one say to that?

What would he do if he actually had to make that choice?

His heart slammed against his chest wall.

"We can't ignore the reality of our situation," Ethan continued. "Sounds like we have a workable possibility on the table, and if we don't figure something out soon, we could lose it all. The family needs to weigh in on this."

Evan's jaw tightened, anger and fear twisting in his gut. "You saying you want to take this offer?"

"Of course not," Ethan said firmly. "But we need options, not ultimatums." He turned to fully face him. "And we need Jessica, so don't go pissing her off. I know how much this land means to you. To all of us. And I'll fight right alongside you for it. But we have to be smart."

Ethan's steady voice and unwavering support eased some of the turmoil in Evan's chest. He sighed, shoulders slumping. "I know. I just... I feel like I'm failing Dad, failing our family."

"Shut up, man. That's not true. And to be honest, I'm tired of hearing you sing that same damn song all the time. You have failed no one. Got it? Now buck the hell up and let's figure this thing out."

"Wow. Thanks, little brother." Evan managed a faint smile. However bleak things seemed, Ethan always gave him hope—even with sarcasm.

"I'm only two minutes younger, so let's just call it even."

Evan chuckled. "Alright."

"Come on." Ethan tilted his head toward the door. "Jessica is sitting out on the porch. Let's take her down to her car and maybe you can make amends during the ride to the main house. But no canoodling, got that?"

As much as Evan would like to canoodle with Jessica, he wasn't about to take that path right now, nor did he think she would let him. "No, you go on. Thanks for taking her down. I need to stay up here and clear my head. I'll bring the horses down later this morning."

Ethan backed away, eyeing him for a moment. "Alright. You know best."

He headed out of the barn, but Evan called out again and stopped him. "Ethan?"

"Yeah?"

"You be around later? When I get back?"

Ethan nodded. "Sure."

"Good. Let's talk. I mean, seriously discuss everything."

Their gazes met and held. Nothing else needed to be said.

Which means more to you, the ranch or Jessica?

Chapter Fourteen

Monday morning, Jessica sat in her car outside the bank, gripping the steering wheel. The clock on the dashboard read seven-fifty-eight, just two minutes until she had to be in her office, and only hours until she had to face Charles Short and Mr. Lance Nelson. She'd be hard pressed to explain why the MacKays hadn't accepted Gage Parker's offer—or perhaps more directly, why she hadn't told them about it.

Of course, that point could be considered moot at this stage of the game. Gage Parker had taken matters into his own hands and called Evan himself.

Why would he do that?

While her meeting with her boss, and her proposal, wasn't until two that afternoon, she still dreaded going inside, her stomach churning with anxiety.

Yesterday, driving away from Sweet Grass Ranch, her thoughts rambled with indecision. She knew she couldn't convince Evan to sell, and she wasn't convinced that selling was the right thing to do. Not when it meant destroying a family. But the bank expected results. Expected her to do whatever it took to get the MacKays to pay off their loans. She had no clue which direction she would take.

With a sigh, she dropped her forehead against the steering wheel. She understood why Evan was fighting so hard against selling—and why he had gotten angry with her. If it had been her family's ranch, she would have done the same.

But she had a job to do. Mr. Nelson had made it clear—get the MacKays to sell and pay off their debt, by any means necessary. And to him, that meant accepting Gage Parker's offer.

She had to convince him otherwise.

Working well into the night, she had prepared two separate and different proposals.

Plan One, was simply selling out to Gage Parker, and the MacKays moving on with their lives, debts paid—but with no home and no land and no immediate way of making a living. In the plus column, they would have the funds to start over.

Plan Two was the messier plan, comprised of the partnership with Nate Brave Eagle, along with the selling of a parcel of the ranch. Whether that was the cabin and surrounding acres or another parcel, remained to be seen. She wasn't going to make decisions for the MacKays about what land to sell, only that they needed to sell enough to cover most or all of their debt. After assessing their other assets that could also sell—the stock business, the herd, and so on—she thought she could make it work.

The thing was, she knew Mr. Nelson would not agree to Plan Two unless the numbers were right.

So, for her ace in the hole, she decided to do something she never did when pitching an idea to a bank manager—play on his emotions and sideline the bottom-line numbers.

"Let's see how it works," she whispered.

It was a risk.

As she sat there trying to work up the courage to go in,

Jessica couldn't help but think of the anguish in Evan's eyes when they had argued.

Could she go through with Mr. Nelson's demands if it came to that? Even if it meant destroying Evan's family and everything they had built?

She reached for her briefcase full of Sweet Grass Ranch files and exited the car. She had six hours until her meeting—all the time she had to review the work she'd done, and make sure she was on the right track.

Her pulse pounded as she walked the concrete sidewalk toward the bank, nervous but resolute. For the first time in years, Jessica felt unsure whether she was doing the right thing.

Abruptly, she stopped, staring at the Cattlemens Bank sign etched into the glass windows on the building. She would do what was right, no matter what.

But if she was wrong, what would it cost her?

Her job?

Evan's love?

Evan—did he love her? Or was he buttering her up just to get on her good side? He'd more or less accused her of the same. Hadn't he?

For a fleeting moment, she realized she did not know where things stood between her and Evan—and suddenly, it was important that she find out.

* * *

Evan looked up when the back door opened and his two younger brothers, Aaron and Aiden, stepped inside. He and Ethan were sharing their morning coffee at the kitchen table while Brandley put the finishing touches on a breakfast casserole and slid it in the oven.

"Morning boys," she said, nodding to them.

Aaron slipped next to her and gave her a quick peck on the cheek. "Ah, I love the smell of bacon on a woman," he teased.

Brandley swiped at him with a dishtowel, laughing. "Oh, shut up. Get some coffee and have a seat at the table."

"Grab me a cup too," Aiden tossed out.

"Your legs broke?"

Aiden rolled his eyes, stepped to the counter, and pulled down a mug from the cabinet.

Evan took another sip of his coffee, glancing at Ethan. His twin's eyes were serious, and Evan knew the next few minutes were not going to be easy, but necessary.

Aaron stood at the coffeemaker, looking out the window. "Is that Dylan coming up the road?"

"Probably." Evan set down his cup. "He worked the night shift last night. Talked to him earlier. He was on his way home."

The younger twins sat at the table, looking across at the older two. A couple of silent minutes passed while they sipped their brew.

"So, what's up?" Aiden said.

Again, Evan glanced at Ethan. "Let's wait until Dylan is here."

"Well, he's here, walking up to the porch." Brandley glanced out the window and tossed the dishtowel on the counter. "I'm going to go check on the baby."

"You coming back?" Ethan asked.

She paused a moment, looking at her husband. "No. I'm leaving this discussion to the brothers. This is on all of you."

Ethan dipped his head in a half-nod.

"The casserole doesn't come out for forty-five minutes. I'll check back in then."

"We can handle it, Brandley, if you're busy," Evan told her.

She gave him a smile and left the kitchen.

Aaron and Aiden exchanged glances. "What was that all about?" Aaron shifted in his seat.

The back door flew open again and Dylan stepped over the threshold. "Man, it's getting chilly out there." He burst inside, shrugged out of his jacket, and hung it on a hook by the door. He placed his hat on a shelf on the other side. Turning, he made eye contact with Evan, and stepped forward, pulling out a kitchen chair. "Alright. What's going on?"

"That's what I just asked." Aaron directed his attention to Dylan.

"We have a situation," Ethan began. "And we need to decide. Today."

Evan's insides quivered like a rabbit on the receiving end of a shotgun. He'd hoped to never have this discussion, but there it was. And maybe he'd been wrong all along.

No use sugar-coating or pussyfooting around.

"We've had an offer to buy the ranch, lock, stock, and barrel."

No one said anything, just stared.

"The offer is substantial. Ethan and I feel like this is not a decision to make without everyone's input. We talked to Mom and Sarah this morning, and we know how they feel. Now, we want the three of you to weigh in."

"Just give it to us straight," Dylan said.

"Gage Parker wants to buy the ranch. His offer is twenty million dollars. Now, Brandley did some of the math last night. Given what we owe to the bank, any fees for selling, splitting the profit seven ways—which is what Mom said to do—each of us would walk away in the ballpark of a million dollars plus." He eyed them, watching their expressions. "Now, that sounds like a lot of money, but let's be honest here, most of us know nothing about anything but ranching, so we'd have to completely start over. A million dollars doesn't get each of us very far."

Dylan drummed his fingers on the table. "Unless we pool our resources and buy another ranch."

"But would that put us back in the same predicament?" Aiden scratched his head.

"Maybe. Maybe not. We would just have to be smarter about it. Thing is, maybe not all of us want to do that."

"Who doesn't?"

The brothers glanced around the table at each other.

Evan leaned forward, looking at Aaron and Aiden. "I figured maybe the two of you would strike out on your own. You're young and could find a new path. You need to think about this."

Aaron shook his head. "Nothing to think about for me. I can't imagine doing anything but ranching."

"Which means you would both need to give up rodeo. We would need all hands on deck."

Dylan slowly nodded. "I can cut back to part time at the Sheriff's office so I can work more on the ranch. I know I said that before, but suddenly, I feel more invested."

Evan nudged Dylan's arm. "Now, I appreciate that, but that's a down the road discussion. First, we all need to decide, right here and now. Are we all in favor of selling the ranch to Gage Parker? He wants an answer by tomorrow morning."

"Wait." Aaron put up a hand. "Do we know what Gage wants to do with the ranch? Is he going to run cattle over it?"

Evan took a breath. "We don't know. And honestly, we shouldn't think about that because that's where we always get into trouble."

Aiden stood. "But what if he wants to turn the place into a hotel? A casino? A vacation destination? Or a dude ranch? How could we stop that?"

Evan closed his eyes. "We can't. Once we sell, we have no voice. It's his. I'm sure he's weighed all the options and contacted the proper local authorities to see what he can do with this land. Once we sign, we can't stop it."

"Then maybe we don't sign," Aaron said.

But Dylan interjected. "And maybe we do. Evan is right. Once it's not our ranch any longer, Gage Parker can do any damn thing he wants with the land."

Ethan stood. "I think we're putting the cart before the horse and borrowing trouble here. Sure, Parker is a hotel billionaire. He also loves his ranches and has thousands of acres outside Billings. He values ranch land as much as the next rancher, so I doubt he's going to do anything other than raise cattle."

"But we don't know that for sure."

"We don't." Ethan gave his brothers a good stare down. "And frankly, we may not have a choice, so that's a situation we may need to get comfortable with."

* * *

Jessica's fingers flew across the keyboard. She was determined and focused, putting the finishing touches on her proposals. When her desk phone rang, she glanced at the caller I.D., and sighed. Quickly checking the time—*the morning is getting away from me*—she pushed the button for the speakerphone. "Yes, Mr. Short?"

"Ms. Chase, I need a word. Could you come to my office, please?"

She glanced at her watch. She needed at least another hour to finish. "Of course. Right after lunch?"

"Right now."

"But I—"

"Now, please."

She swallowed. "I'm on my way."

This can't be good.

With a deep breath, she rose from her desk and headed for his office down the hall. His administrative assistant gave her a nod as she passed her desk. Mr. Short's glare met hers as she crossed the threshold and moved into his office. The afternoon sunlight filtered through the window blinds, casting shadows across his face, so it was difficult to discern from his expression just how serious the meeting might turn out to be.

"Please close the door behind you and have a seat." He gestured toward a leather chair opposite his desk.

"Is there a problem?"

She maintained a steady gaze despite the unease creeping up her spine. Crossing the room, she focused on the polished surface of his mahogany desk, the neat stacks of papers, and the shiny brass nameplate displaying his title. Her heart raced in her chest as she grappled with the conflicting emotions surging within her—she had to maintain her composure.

"Word has reached me..." he began, leveling his gaze, "that you've been spending time with Evan MacKay outside of your work responsibilities."

Jessica's cheeks flushed with embarrassment—*why is this your concern?* "I've spent time at the ranch, that is true. I've met with the family to hear their concerns, had a tour of the facilities, and I've had discussions with Brandley MacKay, their accountant."

"But you've also visited the ranch in a more social way. Isn't that right?"

"Excuse me?"

"You attended their barbecue last week."

"Well, yes, I did, at Connie MacKay's invitation." *And your point is?*

"And apparently, you were there for most of this past weekend."

Now, this is getting ridiculous. "First, I don't see where that is any of your concern, Mr. Short. And secondly, are you having me stalked?"

He dismissed her last question and lowered his gaze. "If your personal life interferes with your decision making here at the bank, that is my concern."

Oh. That's the issue? "I assure you, Mr. Short, my professional judgment has not been compromised."

Mr. Short leaned forward, his fingers laced together. "Jessica, I must emphasize the importance of keeping the Sweet Grass Ranch account in good standing. Our reputation is on the line."

"Of course, sir." She nodded, feeling the weight of her superior's words. "I understand that completely."

"Then you also understand," he continued, "that your personal emotions cannot interfere with your responsibilities at this bank. You must handle this account with precision and professionalism, regardless of any entanglements."

Entanglements? Jessica swallowed, her throat suddenly parched. "Mr. Short, my focus is on the success of this account and the bank. I have never allowed my personal feelings to dictate how I manage my work." *I haven't. Have I?* Suddenly, she wasn't so certain.

"Very well." His eyes narrowed as if searching for any hint of doubt in her words. "See that this situation doesn't become a problem."

"Absolutely." Jessica promised, her resolve strengthening as she met his gaze once more. "I will navigate this task with professionalism and clarity and ensure that the best possible outcome is achieved for all parties involved."

"That's all we ask. Thank you."

With a nod, Jessica stood and left his office, her mind racing with conflicting thoughts as she returned to her desk. She had never considered her growing affection for Evan a liability, and she would not let it cloud her judgment when it came to the ranch. The stakes were too high, both professionally and personally.

On her way back to her office, she paused for a moment, gazing out the large window that framed the Main Street Square of Rapid City below, the Black Hills silhouetted in the background. Cities were fine, but for the first time in her adult life, she had to admit she preferred ranch life.

She'd been running from her past for years. Hadn't she?

Her thoughts drifted to Evan's hands, his soft touch, his fingertips grazing over her body. His kisses, long and sweet and tender—and then later, passionate and heated and all-consuming. She'd loved how their bodies had collided; fit together like they were meant to be. How the thrill of his warmth wrapping around her made her never want to leave his arms.

Footsteps behind her pulled her out of her reverie, and she glanced to see a couple heading toward the elevator.

"Focus," she whispered, shaking off the memory and taking a deep breath. "You have work to do."

In her office, she stared at the proposal on the computer screen in front of her, and the stacks of notes on her desk. The words blurred as her thoughts returned to Evan, but she steeled herself, resolving to compartmentalize her feelings and focus solely on her duties as the bank loan manager for the Sweet Grass Ranch account.

She had to separate herself from the sentiment of her task, keep the balance between personal emotions and professional duties. Clarity and professionalism, she'd told Mr. Short. Right.

"Back to work," Jessica murmured, picking up her pen with determination.

Her eyes scanned the fine print of a financial document, evaluating each line with renewed vigor. As she meticulously reviewed her proposal, her Plan Two, she took great care to ensure that it did not include the complete sale of the ranch. The thought of Evan losing his home and livelihood was almost unbearable, and she would do everything in her power to prevent it.

A coworker called out from her doorway, breaking her concentration. "Hey. We're heading out for lunch if you want to join us."

"Thanks, but I'll pass today," she replied without lifting her gaze from the papers. "I'm prepping for a meeting. Enjoy your lunch."

"Suit yourself."

As the office chatter in the hallway subsided, Jessica dove deeper into her task. Putting her phone on "do not disturb," she reviewed financial statements, analyzed market trends, made a few phone calls, and scrutinized every potential solution that could save the ranch without compromising her professional integrity. Her pen danced across the page, filling it with detailed notes and carefully calculated figures.

The minutes bled together, but Jessica remained steadfast in her efforts. Finally, she signed her name at the bottom of the proposal with a flourish.

"Done," she whispered, leaning back in her chair. The weight of her responsibility still pressed heavily on her shoulders, but she had done everything within her power to secure the future of Sweet Grass Ranch.

All she could do was wait for fate to play its hand... And hope her heart would not betray her.

Chapter Fifteen

Thoughts of Evan still spinning in her head, Jessica allowed herself a moment to indulge in the bittersweet ache of longing that went with her growing feelings for him—and contemplated whether it had been a mistake to spend the night with him. He was a tender, gentle lover when she needed it, and he was passionate and extremely sexy when she needed that, too. She had a feeling what she'd experienced with Evan over the weekend was only a taste of what could be between them.

But they had argued, and some things said were rather hurtful. While she could get past that, could he? Stubborn, grumpy cowboy. Would they be able to settle things enough in their external lives, to move forward emotionally and physically?

She hoped so. Wanted to.

But first things first.

Nearly thirty minutes before her two o'clock meeting with Charles Short, she paced her office, pondering that notion. But just as quickly as the emotions overcame her, she shook them off to focus on the task at hand.

"Maintain professional distance," she murmured. "Focus on the account, not the man."

"Jessica?" Mr. Short's voice broke through the now-silent office hallway, jolting her from her thoughts. He stuck his head inside her office door. "Nelson wants us in his office right away."

"But it's not two yet."

"Now."

Her heart skipped a beat, nerves prickling up her spine as she gathered her proposals and strode down the hallway. She met Mr. Short at the door, which stood open, revealing the no-nonsense Lance Nelson sitting behind a heavy desk, his hands folded in front of him.

"Come in. Close the door." His voice crackled, rather harsh and gravelly, like that of a long-time smoker. Jessica slipped inside and pulled the door closed behind her, feeling the weight of his scrutiny.

He pointed to a chair across from the desk and to Mr. Short's left. She settled into the leather seat.

"Ms. Chase," he began, narrowing his eyes, "this situation with Sweet Grass Ranch has dragged on long enough. Wrap the sale up today, or I'll have no choice but to remove you from the account."

Her chest tightened, anger and fear mingling within. She couldn't let another loan manager take over—not when she had poured herself into finding a solution. But she also knew that, despite her best efforts, convincing Evan to sell was impossible, nor was it in his best interest.

"Mr. Nelson," she said, her voice steady even as her heart raced. "I've put together a proposal which outlines a plan to secure the future of Sweet Grass Ranch without selling the entire ranch. The MacKays would keep their land and their livelihood, and the debt to the bank would be paid in full." She placed the file on his desk. "I would like to walk through it with the two of you." She glanced at Charles Short.

"We have an offer on the ranch. A good one," Nelson interjected. "Gage Parker is hot to buy. No need to review."

She sucked in a breath. "With all due respect, sir, I think the MacKays deserve for us to look at all options." She placed her fingertips on the proposal. "This plan includes selling off a parcel to Gage Parker, and also includes a potential partnership between the MacKays and Nate Brave Eagle, as well as an investment from Mr. Parker. I spoke with him this afternoon. It's a plan that he could get behind—"

Mr. Nelson put up his hand. "Stop. Enough. Obviously, you do not understand what I am saying here."

"But...."

"Ms. Chase. The deal is done. Wrap it up, nice and clean. Your proposal sounds rather messy. Right Short?" He looked at Charles, whose eyes grew round.

"Yes, sir."

Blinking, she stared straight ahead. "What?"

"The MacKays have agreed to sell."

Shaking her head, she looked at her boss, who shrugged.

"What? No. That's not possible."

"It is entirely possible. They are on their way now to discuss the details. When they get here, finish your job."

Suddenly, her mouth felt as parched as the high desert in August. "I can't do that," she told him.

"And why?"

"Because I don't..." *Agree.*

"Ms. Chase. It's a simple matter, really. Get the MacKays in a room, explain the deal and the procedure, get their signatures on the required documents, and call it a day. Mission accomplished."

No. I can't.

Her head swirled and her tummy flipped, a queasiness settling in her abdomen. She'd worked so hard. She knew Evan didn't want to sell. Why in the world did they turn the tables on her? On themselves?

Had he given up on her? Because of their argument?

Because they slept together?

Suddenly, she felt humiliated and helpless.

"Jessica?"

She stood. "My apologies to you both. I realize this is unexpected and extremely unprofessional, but right now, I can't help that. I can't do what you are asking me to do."

Lance Nelson rose behind his desk. To be honest, she was certain this was the first time she'd ever seen him do anything but sit behind it. Leaning closer, his fists parked on the shiny glass top, his knuckles bulging, he peered at her. "Excuse me?"

Just get it over with.

"I quit." Her words were firm, her resolve unwavering. Dizziness set in and her legs suddenly grew weak. Bracing herself against the desk, she glanced into the faces of both men.

What have I done?

"You don't mean that. Now, I'm going to just shake that off and forget you said it. Calm yourself down and get ready to meet the MacKays in an hour and get them to sign on the dotted line."

I've failed them, and they gave it all up. Gave up on me?

That hurt her heart more than anything.

"I'm sorry. No." She turned, stumbling toward the door. She'd had enough. She'd tried and tried to make things work, so that the MacKays didn't have to sell the ranch. And now? They took the freaking deal?

"Jessica!" Mr. Nelson called after her, but she didn't look back.

Looking back never got her anywhere.

* * *

An hour later, Evan sat in the small conference room at Cattlemens Bank, along with all four of his brothers, and Ethan's wife, Brandley. He was told they would get his mother and Sarah on speakerphone, along with Gage Parker, when the loan officer arrived.

Jessica, he assumed.

Their decision would be quite a surprise to her, and he wondered if she knew already. When he'd not been able to reach her earlier, he'd called Lance Nelson and had discussed with him. He'd thought about calling her on the way into Rapid but figured it best to chat with her face to face.

Besides, they'd not talked since they'd argued, so he had a couple of things to settle.

He'd practiced what he wanted to say all the way into town, insisting he drive alone so he could talk out loud in the truck cab. He'd apologize, first, for being a horse's ass. And then he'd explain what the family had discussed and decided upon.

But before that, perhaps he should thank her for all she'd done.

No, that might not work. She might think he was finished with her, thanking her and sending her on her way.

That's the last thing he wanted.

When Charles Short burst into the conference room, carrying a stack of folders and a bottle of water, and sitting across the table from them, his radar suddenly went up.

He'd worked with Charles frequently, before the guy was moved up into a supervisory position, so they knew each other well—well enough that Evan called him Chuck.

"Surprised to see you, Chuck."

The loan officer nodded, setting the stack of folders to his left—and to Evan's right. He reached out to shake everyone's hands, one by one. "It's good to see all of you here this afternoon. I realize this is a sensitive situation, so I'll try to make it as painless as possible."

Evan leaned forward, studying him. Chuck appeared nervous and was sweating around his temples. *Where is Jessica?*

Chuck Short continued, "Now, we'll get started as soon as I get the others on speaker." He fiddled with the conference phone in the center of the table. "Let's see. I'll need to do a two-way call. Do you have Sarah's number?"

"I do," Brandley said. "I'll write it down for you."

"Excellent."

Evan glanced at Ethan and fidgeted in his chair. Looking at Chuck, he asked, "When is Jessica coming?"

Chuck didn't look up from his task. "She isn't, sorry to say."

"What?" Both Ethan and Evan chorused the word.

Chuck Short forced a sigh, then looked up at the group. "Jessica is no longer employed with Cattlemens. I'll be taking over to close out the account."

Immediately, Evan knew something was wrong. "Wait. What?" He stood. "Where is she?"

"She left about an hour ago."

Evan perused the faces of his family staring back at him. They all had questions, he could tell. Something wasn't right, and suddenly, the bank deal didn't feel right either.

Chuck leaned back, his left hand landing on the stack of folders. Evan noticed his forefinger bobbing up and down on the top folder... As if he were pointing to something he wanted Evan to see.

Whoa. Maybe he did.

Evan leaned closer, reading the label on the outside of the folder. "May I see this?" he said, reaching for it.

"Of course. It's something Jessica put together before she left."

Evan met Chuck's gaze and held it for a few seconds. Then he looked to the folder again and read the label: *Sweet Grass Ranch Proposal #2, Prepared by Jessica Chase.*

"Have you read this?"

Chuck nodded. "Just in the last hour, after she left."

"And what do you think?"

"I think you need to read it. All of you."

Evan flipped through the pages, thinking. Then lifting his gaze, and after looking over his family, he turned to Chuck. "Did she get fired?"

"No. She left of her own accord."

"Why?"

Chuck let out another sigh. "I'll probably get fired for this, but so be it. If she can put her neck on the line, then so can I. That girl has guts, I tell you."

Panic surged up inside Evan. "What happened?"

"Nelson was trying to force her into doing something she didn't want to do, which was get you to sell and tie up the deal. He wouldn't let her review the proposal with us. He gave her an ultimatum."

At that point, Ethan stood up, too. "And she quit for us?"

"I think she quit," Chuck said, "because she felt like she'd failed all of you."

"That's ridiculous," Brandley said, also standing.

Saying nothing, Dylan, Aaron, and Aiden stood too. That's when Evan knew he and his family were in solidarity. His mother had already said she was fine with whatever they wanted to do, and Sarah would be as well.

Evan gave Chuck his attention. "May we take this?"

"Of course."

"Good. We'll get with you soon as we review. We're not signing anything today." He looked at his family. "Right?"

"Absolutely," Ethan said.

"Right," the younger twins echoed.

"I'm good." Dylan picked up his hat. "Time to be heading out, I say."

Brandley picked up her folders. "Right behind you all."

"Great," Evan eased his gaze over to Chuck. "We'll let you get back to your day and will be in touch very soon."

Chuck shrugged. "Hope I'll still be here." He laughed nervously.

On the way out of the building, the MacKays were mostly silent until they approached their vehicles parked on the street. Evan turned to Ethan. "Call Mom and Sarah and let them know what happened, and that we'll call them back soon as we get to the ranch. Let's all go over this together."

"I'll do that on the drive back."

"Great."

Turning to Brandley, he asked, "Do you have Jessica's number?"

"I think I have her cell phone."

"Good. Because all I have is her office number."

Ethan rolled his eyes. "Good God, man. You are pitiful."

He shrugged it off, looking at Brandley. "Text me her cell phone ASAP. Okay?"

"Doing it right now."

"Good. I'll give her a quick call. Let's get home and review this proposal."

* * *

The setting sun cast long shadows across the highway as Jessica drove out of South Dakota on I-90, crossing into Wyoming. After leaving Mr. Nelson's office, she'd stopped long enough at her office to grab her purse and the only other personal thing she had there—the picture of her parents and grandparents on her desk.

After a quick trip to her apartment, changing clothes and packing a small bag, she gassed up her Tahoe and headed west. She wasn't sure where she would end up, but it didn't matter. Wyoming was home—and right now, she needed home.

Her heart ached for the MacKays—and for herself. She'd wanted to do good things at Cattlemens. Had high hopes for herself there, possibly making a career working with ranchers. All of that was done. She'd failed. And she doubted she'd ever work in the banking industry again.

The SUV was quiet, perfect for thinking. She didn't listen to music, or an audiobook, or a podcast, like she usually would do. After two calls from the bank, which she didn't pick up, and another from Evan, which surprised her, she turned her phone off. She didn't pick up his call, either, letting it go to voice mail.

She was not ready to talk to him. Not yet.

Instead, while the miles of pavement droned on under her wheels, she used the silence in the truck cab to mull over anything that came to mind, from the events of the past few weeks to her tentative relationship with Evan, to years past when she'd left Wyoming for Boston—and how all of that made her feel.

Had her present situation enhanced her emotional connection to the past? Had her past shaped her future, and maybe even the decision to quit her job?

What now?

She pulled into a roadside motel somewhere between Gillette and Buffalo. The building sported a blinking, half lit, glowing neon vacancy sign in front. She got a room for the night. Not a five-star hotel by any stretch, but the sheets were clean and so was the bathroom, so she'd call that a win. It was only after she had brushed her teeth and was ready to slip into bed, that she realized she'd not eaten all day. Too late. She'd find a good place for breakfast.

When she woke the next morning, the sun streaming through the streaked picture window between the uneven curtains, Jessica knew exactly where she was headed.

If only she could remember how to get there. She knew she had to go south, catching I-25 at Buffalo. She'd follow her heart from there.

Hours later, and after several wrong turns, Jessica felt a mournful thud land deep in the pit of her gut as she turned onto a familiar ranch road. It had been over twenty years since she'd traveled this path. She had no idea what she would find in the end, but she wasn't going to stop for anything.

The crunch of sand and gravel beneath her tires was a haunting reminder of just how far she had come—and of how much she had lost. Gripping the steering wheel so tight her knuckles ached, she stared ahead, steeling herself for what might come next.

As she drove, her mind wandered, and the pang in her stomach escalated as her mind raced with images and pictures, laced with emotion and melancholy, from her past—the picnics outside on the old oak table under the tree, the summers of riding Starshine over the prairie, the cottonwoods along the creek turning yellow in the fall, early mornings letting the horses out then watering and feeding them and mucking out the stalls.

The songs in the kitchen. Fresh-baked apple pies in the windowsill.

Her grandfather scolding her for staying out too late, riding.

She smiled. His scoldings were so harmless.

Home. It all spoke to her of home.

Then she thought of the MacKays.

It pained her to think that she had failed, that she was

responsible for smashing their hopes for the future, for them losing their home. A lump formed in her throat at the thought, but she swallowed it down.

One day, she would call them and apologize.

One day.

Not today.

There was nothing she could do about it. The sting was too real. The best thing for everyone was for her to get out, and stay out, of their lives—at least for the time being.

Perhaps it was time to build a new life.

Chapter Sixteen

They all sat around the kitchen table with the one copy of Jessica's ten-page proposal spread out before them. Evan would read a page, then pass it along to Ethan, who passed it along to Dylan, and then to Aaron and Aiden. Brandley read over Ethan's shoulder, making a comment once in a while. But mostly, they were silent while reading.

Ethan wanted them to each come up with their own conclusions.

When the pile of papers was finally stacked up beside Aiden, Evan gave the crew a look, called his mother who was waiting at Sarah's, on his cell. He placed the phone in the center of the table and turned on the speaker.

"Can you hear us all okay, Mom?"

The brothers all said hello to their mother.

"Fine. We can hear you fine."

"Great."

"Tell us about Jessica's proposal."

Evan glanced about again at his brothers. "Well, looks like she did a lot of legwork for us to partner with Nate and also Gage Parker. Here's the deal in a nutshell. Instead of buying us out, she negotiated a deal with Parker to purchase the north parcel of land which backs up to the Caldwell ranch, which he apparently plans to buy this week. She also worked out the lease agreement with Nate for grazing land. There are some provisions for future partnership on a bison herd, and an investment from Gage into what would be a new business."

Ethan shifted in his seat. "Looks like to me that Nate, Parker, and the MacKays would be equal partners in this new venture. According to Jessica's proposal, Gage would need someone here to manage his new ranch, so we have that option. Details to be worked out."

"And we have access to all of the Caldwell ranch grazing land too," Aaron added.

"Which means we could possibly have enough land to run both cattle and bison," Dylan said. "With Nate's ranch, ours, and Gage's, we'd be controlling over twenty-thousand acres."

"Sounds like a lot of work to me," Aiden admitted.

"To tell you the truth," Evan said. "I'm looking forward to the possibilities. Mom, you've been quiet. What do you think?"

She was silent for a few seconds, but then said, "I think Jessica is brilliant. Is she there? I want to talk to her."

Evan stared at the tabletop. The room fell silent. "No, she's not here. We'll have to talk to her later."

"Oh sure," his mother said.

His family chattered on for several minutes, and while he heard their words, he wasn't really listening to what they were saying. His mind had wandered off to Jessica and how he wanted her by his side to celebrate her work, and to thank her for all she had done for them.

But mostly, he wanted to hold her close and kiss her silly.

"So, we're all in agreement then?" Ethan nudged Evan, yanking him out of his daydream.

Evan jerked a nod. "Yes. Of course. I'm all in."

"We are doing this?"

He nodded again. "We are doing this."

"Good," Connie said. "The baby is crying so Sarah left. I'm going to go check with her now and tell her the news. Love you boys. Talk later. Bye!"

Evan clicked off his phone and pulled it toward him.

Brandley leaned over Ethan's shoulder, toward Evan, and said softly. "Go call her again. Now."

He shook his head. "She's not answering, Brandley. I've already left too many messages."

"And you'll leave more before she caves in. She has to pick them up eventually. Call her."

Staring at the phone, he knew he should. He just didn't know if he had it in him to leave her another pitiful voice mail.

He stood and slipped the phone into his shirt pocket. "Maybe later. I'm going for a ride. When I get back, if we all feel the same, then let's call the bank and get this thing rolling."

* * *

The old ranch house came into view as Jessica passed under the sign. *Western Hills Cattle Ranch* were the words burned into the wood across the top. It wasn't a new sign. It was the same sign that stood there when her grandparents owned the farm. Seeing it gave her a pang, but she also smiled, knowing that some things do stay the same.

She drove slowly toward the collection of buildings—the house, a barn, several outbuildings, the corral offside the barn, and another behind the house. She took it all in, emotion stirring in her chest. It was mid-morning, and the sun climbed the sky in the east, casting down rays of sunshine over the scene, growing ever more real before her.

She slowed and placed her foot on the brake as she crossed

through an open gate with a cattle guard and sat staring at the house.

Whoever had bought it hadn't let the ranch lie fallow and in decay, as she'd pictured it so many times in her head. She didn't know why she thought that, because why would anyone buy a ranch and let it rot? Perhaps in her childish mind, her fourteen-year-old mind, that's all she could imagine. For twenty years, she'd imagined this place the same as she left it, only worse.

But that wasn't the case.

Someone had kept the place up. And there were children playing in the yard. Two little girls in flowery sundresses took turns swinging on a tire swing hanging from the old tree in the yard—in exactly the spot where her grandparents' picnic table used to sit. Rolling down her window, she could hear their laughter. The melody of their giggles fell sweetly on her heart.

She turned off the engine and left the car.

A woman exited the house and stood on the porch, shielding her eyes from the sun. Jessica slowly approached. The little girls stopped playing and ran toward her.

"Hi!" the smaller one said. "You visit?"

"Emily, don't bother the lady." The woman, the girls' mother, she assumed, moved down the porch steps toward her. "May I help you? Are you lost?"

I suppose I am, in a way. "Yes, perhaps. I... I'm sorry. I don't mean to intrude. I just wanted to see the ranch."

The woman cocked her head and studied her for a few seconds. "Oh? Are you interested in cattle? Because that's what we do here."

"I know." Jessica nodded toward the pasture. "I can see that." Pausing for a moment, she then blurted out. "I grew up here. On this ranch."

The woman stepped closer. "You did?"

"Yes. With my grandparents."

The woman studied her. "Wait. Jessica? Are you...?"

Taken aback for a moment, all she could do was blink and stare at the woman. After a minute, she said, "I am. How did you know?"

The woman took another step. "You don't remember me, do you? I'm Annabelle Walker. Anna. Anna Summers, now. I married Johnny Summers. We were in the same class in school, you and me. I lived right down the road, Mile High Ranch. My parents still own it. We rode the school bus together in elementary school."

The surprise caught Jessica's breath. "Anna? Oh, my goodness. I remember!"

Anna touched her hand. "My parents bought this ranch when it went up for auction all those years ago. It neighbors theirs. When Johnny and I married, we moved here and created our own cattle company."

Just knowing that made Jessica's heart soar. "Oh, Anna. I'm so happy for you." She glanced about, her mind wandering. "I remember we used to meet at the fence in the back pasture, where the ranches met, over by the creek. I got in so much trouble one day for being late getting back home."

"Me too! Remember that time we went swimming in the creek in our underwear? My goodness, I would tan these girls' hides if they pulled a stunt like that."

Jessica laughed. "I remember that day."

The women embraced, and tears stung Jessica's eyes a little. Anna pulled back. "These are my girls, Emily and Sophie. Johnny's out on the ranch somewhere. You have to come inside so we can catch up. Stay for lunch."

"Oh, I don't want to intrude on your day."

Anna smiled wide. "You are not intruding. Come inside. I have something to give you."

"Really?"

Anna grinned. "Yes. Really."

Jessica followed her into the house, slowly taking in her surroundings. Each step was like a memory, and each memory grew stronger as they went inside and stood in the living room. She turned around, taking in every nook and cranny.

"You've not changed much."

Anna beamed. "We like the vintage look and feel. I couldn't see redoing the woodwork and built-in bookshelves just because they were dated. They were structurally fine and beautiful. A little soap and water and paint and they came alive again."

"I love it. I remember so many things happening in this room." *Holidays. Birthdays. Family get-togethers. Happier times.* She looked ahead, through the archway into the kitchen. "And the kitchen, too. Just the same."

"A few updates here and there, but yes, it's the same."

Slightly overwhelmed, Jessica sat on the sofa. Her grandmother stood at the stove, in her mind's eye, making lunch.

Anna touched her shoulder. "Why don't you sit a bit and just reminisce? I'll get the girls cleaned up a little and fix lunch. Wander around as much as you like."

Looking up, Jessica nodded. "Thank you."

Anna lingered, then said quietly, "I remember when your grandparents' died. I felt so bad for you. Then you were gone. I never knew what happened to you."

"I know. It all happened so fast. I went into foster care."

"Oh, goodness." Anna sat for a minute beside her, then leaned in to give her a hug. "I'm so sorry, Jessica. I never got to say that back then, so I'm saying it now."

Jessica hugged her back. "Thanks, Anna."

"Okay, so let me go do those things. I'll be back in a few minutes."

Falling back against the sofa, Jessica absorbed the ambiance of the house. She wanted to cry, and she didn't. A part of her wanted to laugh hysterically in relief. Seeing the place again was cathartic, and knowing that Anna was living there, making the place a home again, gave her peace. She'd dreamed for years of coming back to buy it, to save it, to make it her home again.

But she didn't have to. Did she?

The old family ranch was already a home—for another family. And it was a beautiful thing. Suddenly, she knew she could put Wyoming behind her. She didn't have to save her grandparents' ranch any longer—they had already saved it.

Little girl giggles and footsteps sounded down the hallway as Emily and Sophie burst into the room. Sophie, the older girl, carried a small box. The moment she saw it, Jessica's heart swelled.

"For you," Sophie said, stepping closer.

Anna stepped into the room and Jessica caught her eye. She could barely see between the tears. "It's my music box," she whispered.

A broad smile spread across Anna's face. "Yes. We found it under—"

"Under the loose board in the floor by the window in my bedroom. It was my hidey-hole."

Annabelle nodded. "Yes."

Jessica took the box from Sophie, set it on her lap, and carefully opened the lid. Music tinkled from the inside and a ballerina dancer spun on her tiny pedestal. With a sigh, Jessica lifted the pictures stacked inside.

"There were a lot of photos scattered in various places throughout the house," Annabelle told her. "In drawers, taped behind doors in kitchen cabinets, on the shelves in closets. I put them all in there for you, hoping one day I would see you again."

Jessica shuffled through the pictures, unable to stop her tears.

"Oh, and be sure to find the necklace in the bottom."

Jerking her head up, Jessica exhaled. "What?"

"Look."

She lifted the photos. Underneath was a tiny gold heart-shaped locket. Jessica fiddled with the tiny clasp to open it, but she knew what was inside, and she was right. "It's my parents," she said, "when they were very young. Before all the trouble."

Anna reached out a hand. "Here. Let me put it on you."

Turning, she let her friend clasp the necklace behind her neck, then she fondled the heart at her throat. "It's tinier than I remember."

"It's beautiful."

Jessica returned her attention to the pictures. There were several of her dad and mom, many more of her grandparents, and a few pictures of her as a very young girl. One of them of her sitting atop Starshine.

After a minute, she looked up at Anna and whispered. "I am so grateful. Thank you."

Anna sat beside her again, folding her into her arms. "Let's not let twenty years go by before we see each other again."

"No. Let's not," she whispered.

"This is your home, Jessica. You are welcome here any time. In fact, stay for a few days? We can catch up."

"I do appreciate it. But let's see...."

Anna searched her eyes. "When you first stepped up toward the house, I thought you looked lost. Now, you don't appear to be at all."

Jessica clasped her hand and squeezed it. For the first time in a long time, she didn't feel lost.

* * *

The atmosphere in the bank conference room was livelier than a week earlier, when Evan thought he was about to sign away his

178

legacy. Glancing about, he took in the smiling faces of his family around him—all of them. His mother and Noah had literally just driven in from Montana. His sister, Sarah, her husband, Cole, and their baby son, Elliot, had arrived two days ago, introducing everyone to their new nephew.

Nate Brave Eagle and Gage Parker rounded out the group.

Chuck Short sat at the head of the table, coordinating all the paperwork. All eyes turned toward the door as Lance Nelson stepped inside the room and sauntered toward an empty chair near the end.

"Don't mind me," he said, waving his hand. "I'm just here to observe and learn more about this new partnership. Chuck will navigate everything for you."

Chuck nodded. "It's a shame that Jessica couldn't be here. This was all her doing, of course."

Connie laid a hand on the table. "Has anyone heard from her?"

No one ventured forth any information.

Evan sat quietly, staring at the slick cherry tabletop.

"I believe Human Resources has been in contact with her," Chuck said. "They might know something, although any of us would be hard-pressed to get information from them—like getting wine out of a rock."

"Let's get on with it," Evan said, a little gruffer than he had intended. He wasn't in the mood to discuss Jessica. This was a happy day, after all. And thinking of Jessica just made him, well, sad.

He'd pined after her for days. It had been over a week since she'd left. He'd tried calling, left more messages, but she never picked up. He'd even searched for information on the Internet about any Chase families in Wyoming but didn't come up with much at all. He didn't dig deep, feeling somewhat like a stalker diving into her personal affairs.

If she didn't want him to know where she was, then who was he to push her?

The thing was, that didn't make his broken heart feel any better.

"Well then, let me reiterate our business here today," Chuck said. He shuffled some more stacks of paperwork in front of him. "We'll handle the parcel sale first, the thousand acres on the back side of the ranch to Gage Parker. This section backs up to the neighboring ranch that Gage bought last week, which gives him quite a bit of land to work with. Everyone agrees this is what you want. Correct?"

Evan glanced at his siblings and mother. They all nodded or responded with a yes.

"Good. We'll start with you, Evan. Sign these papers and then pass them around the table. When they get to Gage, then he will sign as well. We'll file them and get the deed transferred, and that is done."

Connie leaned forward. "And this sale will pay toward how much of our debt?" she asked.

"Well, minus commission fees and taxes, you'll be free and clear."

"And we keep the cabin and acreage there?"

"That's right."

His mother looked shocked, and she turned to Evan. "How could that be?"

"It was all part of Jessica's plan, Mom. Since Gage was buying the Caldwell ranch, he preferred that parcel on the other side of the creek. Jessica worked that out with him last week. We sold the rodeo stock, along with some equipment, and most of the herd. By going into partnership with Nate, we don't need the cattle right now, so we put those funds toward debt first."

"That's right," Chuck explained. "Now, we'll deal with the

partnership agreements, which is what I'm sure you all want to be very clear on."

"Please go on," Connie said.

Evan could tell she was relieved the cabin was not selling.

"Good idea." Chuck stacked up the signed paperwork and handed it off to his assistant.

"Now, the partnership for the bison business between the three parties—the MacKay family, Nate Brave Eagle's Dakota Ranches Bison, and Parker Ranches, Inc. I'll be brief. We have the Limited Liability Company paperwork here to sign, that all of you have reviewed, which forms a new company, Sweet Grass Buffalo. In a nutshell, Nate is supplying the herd, the MacKays are adding new grazing land, along with Parker Ranches, Inc., plus Gage Parker is investing a sum of money in the business for startup costs. The MacKays will manage the old Caldwell ranch, now Gage's, plus their own. The profits division is explained in the paperwork. Does that all sound right?"

"Does to me," Evan said.

Everyone else around the table agreed.

Gage Parker leaned forward. "I'm excited about the future," he paused, glancing around the table, "and I hope all of you are, too. This is an excellent solution."

Beside him, Nate Brave Eagle nodded. "As am I. Together, we are much stronger than separate. Our families, our land, will benefit."

Evan's heart was suddenly full of hope. "I am eager to get started."

"We all are," Dylan added.

"I have a question," Connie said. "Who will oversee the finances? Brandley is busy enough with her own work and the baby now, and this operation looks to be a lot bigger than what she had to deal with before. Plus, Hap was so lackadaisical about the money, and he shared nothing or talked about it, so we didn't know when we were in trouble. I don't want that to happen again. How can we avoid that?"

Lance Nelson stood up and looked at Connie. "Yes, we've discussed that. One reason the bank agreed to this plan was because it was well thought out, and all the parties were equally invested. There is history among everyone here and we trust the work will be done. But you're right, Connie, we want to make sure that the business does not fall into the accounting nightmare that it fell into before, so the bank will recommend an accountant. While your debt is dissolved, there will still be times you'll need to draw against your herd when you're in need of new equipment and such. We'll assign a manager who will oversee everything and work in tandem with the accountant, monitoring the day-to-day expenses."

Connie nodded. "I like the sound of that."

Evan added, "We are all in agreement with this plan, Mom. Gage and Nate too. So that made it easy."

"Good." Connie glanced about, then looked at Lance Nelson. "So, who do you recommend for the accountant?"

Mr. Nelson opened his mouth to speak but was quickly interrupted as Jessica stepped through the conference room door.

"Me," she said.

Everyone redirected their attention her way.

Jessica scanned the room, locking gazes with Evan. "I would like to apply for that position. If you'll have me."

His heart slammed against his chest wall.

Chapter Seventeen

Her heart in her throat, Jessica tentatively stepped inside the conference room, her gaze locked tight with Evan's—like he was the only other person in the room. And honestly, at that moment, she saw no one else.

"I owe you an apology," she said softly.

Evan slowly stood. "No. You owe us nothing. In fact, we owe everything to you."

She took another step. "I ran away. I can explain why."

Little by little, he moved around the table. Her heart thrummed with every inch he grew closer.

"To be honest, all I really want to know is why you came back."

With a deep sigh, Jessica tried to calm her nerves. "I came back," she whispered, "because I think I found my home."

"Oh?"

Evan stood in front of her, staring into her eyes. He took her elbows into his palms and eased closer, looking down at her. "And where is home?" he whispered.

She searched the depths of his eyes, her breathing suddenly

shallow. She grasped his forearms. "Wherever you are," she whispered back.

Evan closed his eyes and tugged her closer. Lowering his head, he touched his forehead to hers and murmured. "I've been a miserable, grouchy cowboy since you left. I'm glad you're back. And I'm sorry we argued."

Jessica cupped her cranky cowboy's face in her hands and smiled. "I'm sorry too. Now, about that job?"

Evan grinned. "I don't know, what do you say folks? Think she's up to the work?"

The entire room exploded behind Evan as they stood and applauded.

"I think that's your answer?"

Jessica tossed back her hair and gave him a saucy grin. "I don't know," she said.

"Oh?"

"I think we may need to seal it with a kiss."

"You do, huh? Right here in front of my family and everyone?"

Jessica grabbed the placket of his shirt and jerked him closer. "Absolutely. Right here, right now."

And before he could worm away, Jessica threw her arms around his neck and dove in for a long, sweet, and oh-so-swoon-worthy kiss. Right in front of them all.

When Evan finally edged back, looking into her eyes, and brushing a few stray hairs from her face, she added, "Kiss me again, cowboy."

* * *

"So, what did the two of you talk about?" Ethan prodded, elbowing Evan in the side.

He ignored his brother, but punched him back, sending the mail skittering over the polished oak kitchen table.

They'd been home about an hour after signing all the paperwork. Jessica stayed to speak with Human Resources at the bank and meet with Short and Nelson to define her new position. They'd chatted briefly, agreeing to meet him at Sweet Grass later that afternoon.

"Quit rough housing at the table. I swear, some days, the two of you are thirteen again." Brandley scolded her husband and his brother. She set a few plates on the table and headed toward the sink. "Good gracious, Evan. It's about time you pull your weight around here and bring home another woman who can help me keep you boys in line."

"Oh, that so? Like, who are you suggesting?"

She glanced out the window. "Like the woman driving up the ranch road right now. Looks like a black Tahoe to me."

"Seriously?"

"Damned straight."

Evan stood and went to the door. His heart was about to explode because he wanted Jessica in his arms again—he might just never let her go. Ever.

"And if you ask me," Ethan shouted out after him. "You better put a ring on it before she realizes what a jerk loser you are."

Evan ignored that remark, too.

Slowly, he exited the house and strolled out onto the porch. Leaning against a post, he waited for the Tahoe to make its way into the parking area. Jessica slowly got out, studied him for a minute, then ambled his way, a tentative smile on her face.

"You lost?" he said.

"Not now."

"That so?"

She stopped at the bottom step. "Yes. I hope I wasn't too bold back there in the bank earlier. I didn't mean to assume...."

He pushed away from the post. "Jessica, make no assumption. I want you here. Besides, your boldness saved our ranch."

She grinned. "When I was gone, I realized where I belong."

"Oh, and how is that?"

She took the two steps up the porch to stand right in front of him. "I have some things to tell you."

"No, me first."

"Okay. What then?"

"You put everything on the line for us, and I don't know how we can ever repay you."

She shook her head, glancing down at the porch. "There is nothing to repay, Evan." She lifted her gaze then and looked into his eyes. "I wanted to save the ranch for you. I only put into words what we discussed, bantered about, but I made them happen. The thing was, Mr. Nelson wouldn't listen."

"So you quit?"

"I had no choice. Besides, there was a side thing going on that I needed to figure out, too."

"Oh?"

She nodded. "Yes. I went back to my grandparents' ranch. I found it."

"And...?"

"It's all good. I can tell you about it later if you want to listen."

"I will always want to listen, sweetheart." He grasped her around the waist, tugging her closer. Pressing his forehead against hers, he whispered, "You didn't say goodbye."

"I know and I'm sorry. I thought I had failed you and your family. I couldn't face the fact that I couldn't save the ranch."

Evan shook his head. "But you did save it. You just didn't know."

"Can you forgive me for running away?"

"You broke my heart, Jessica."

She looked up into his eyes. "Can I try to put it back together?"

"Only one way I know how to do that, sweetheart."

"Oh? And how is that?"

"Kiss me again, Jessica Chase. And this time make it last."

Epilogue

S *even months later…*

Connie MacKay Parker bustled about the kitchen of the family cabin, barking orders to her youngest set of twins, listening to their complaining banter.

"Geez, Mom. Can we take a break?" Aaron grumbled. "My back hurts."

She tossed him a look. "Should have thought about that before you rode that bronc the other night." Grinning, she met his gaze. "Just a few more boxes into the back of the pickup truck and we'll be done. I think we've moved all the big pieces. Right, Aiden?"

"I think so. The moving van is getting full."

She hustled toward the door and looked out. "I knew we should have rented a bigger one, but Noah felt this one would do. Of course, the next thing he'll have to worry about is where we are going to put all this stuff at his house in Montana."

Aaron plopped down on a kitchen chair. "So, once we move the stuff you want out, then we have to move things up from the main house, right?"

"Just a few things." Connie turned and faced her boys. "Evan and Jessica ordered new bedroom furniture which will arrive tomorrow, and the men who deliver will move those in and set everything up. But, Evan wants his bedroom furniture at the main house moved into the second bedroom here. Plus, a few other items." She glanced about the cabin, taking in the ambiance of the place she had loved so much. "Oh, I can't tell you how good it makes me feel to know that Evan and Jessica will be living here."

She sighed, contentment settling over her heart and soul.

"And then we have to go to Jessica's apartment?"

Connie smiled. "Yes. I have her keys. All of her things have to be moved from the apartment to the cabin. They've boxed up most everything."

Aaron laid back in the chair, his long legs stretched out. "Meanwhile, the two of them are lounging around on a beach somewhere in Mexico soaking up the sun."

"It's their honeymoon!" Connie patted his legs and headed into the kitchen. "Now get up. We have a lot to do, and they are home in three days. I want everything to be perfect for them the minute they get back."

Aaron groaned and stood. "Okay, what next?"

"Buck it up, man," Aiden prodded. "It's just a few more boxes. You'll be getting a bigger physical workout once you get to boot camp."

Connie dropped a handful of silverware on the floor.

The boys turned quickly.

She glared at Aiden. "What did you say?"

Aaron punched his brother in the shoulder. "Shit, man. Why did you go and do that?"

"Hey!" Aiden playfully pushed his brother back. "I thought you told her."

"Told me what?" Connie rushed in between them, then turned to Aaron. "Aaron MacKay, what have you gone and done?"

Her heart beat wildly against her throat. "Aaron?"

Her youngest son peered into her eyes. "I talked with Ethan about it, Mom. A lot. I've been floundering these past few years since high school. It's what I need to do, want to do. I joined the Navy."

The literal breath whooshed out of Connie's lungs. It was true that both of her youngest sons couldn't seem to get settled. She glanced at Aiden. "You too?"

He shook his head. "No ma'am. I'm staying here on the ranch."

"Good," she whispered. Gradually, she lowered herself to a kitchen chair and sat. "Oh, Aaron...."

He crouched in front of her. "I want to be a SEAL, Mom. Like Ethan. I want to serve my country and protect our way of life."

Connie didn't know when she'd been so proud, or so scared. The years rolled back to the day Ethan had told her he had enlisted—how frightened she'd been for him then. And how worried and terrified she'd been during every mission he'd ever been on and when he was injured and she couldn't get to him. Then, the long days and months after he came home, battered, beaten down, and depressed.

She stared into Aaron's youthful eyes, and wanted to stare into them for as long as she could. Because she knew when all was said and done, he wouldn't be her young, innocent, bronc- and bull-riding boy any longer.

Aaron took her hands in his. "Be proud of me, Mom," he whispered.

She cupped his face in her palm, tears stinging her eyes. "I am proud of you, Aaron. But I'm scared, too. When do you leave?"

Aaron glanced at his brother. "Next week."

Too soon.

* * *

Hey there! Maddie here. I'm so glad you picked up Evan's story. I certainly hope you enjoyed. Have you read his twin brother, Ethan's story? You can find it wherever you buy your books. Check him out. He's waiting for you!

If you enjoyed Evan, please consider leaving a review wherever you purchased this book—I appreciate it and look forward to your feedback!

More Cowboys!

Scroll on for more cowboy stories in Maddie James' world!

Rock Creek Ranch

The Rancher's Second Chance (Book 1)
Callie (Book 2)
Parker (Book 3)
Leaving Noah (Book 4)

Future releases:
Finn's Lawman
Abby's Secret

The Branded Filly Ranch

Corporate Cowboy (Book 1)
Protecting Sarah (Book 2)

Future release:
Saving Amanda

Remington Ranch, Texas

Jake's Temptation (Book 1)

Sweet Grass Ranch, South Dakota

Ethan: Black Sheep Cowboy (Book 1)
Evan: Kiss Me Again, Cowboy (Book 2)

Future Releases
Aiden: Marry Me, Cowboy (Book 3)
Aaron: The Cowboy's Baby (Book 4)

Colorado Dreamin' Books
Rawhide and Roses (Book 1)
The Cowboy's Secret Baby (Book 2)
Broken (Book 3)

...and more to come!

Do you get my Insider News?

Be the first to get the latest news about my books—new releases, free ebooks, sales and discounts, sneak peeks, and exclusive content! Just add your email address at this link: https://maddiejamesbooks.com/pages/newsletter
Bonus! I'll send you a FREE ebook for signing up.

About Maddie James

Maddie James writes to silence the people in her head—if only they wouldn't all talk at once!

From flirty contemporary romance to darker erotic titles—often mixed with a dash of suspense or a hint of paranormal—Maddie pens stories that often blend a variety of romantic sub-genres. The happily-ever-after, of course, is non-negotiable.

Affaire de Coeur says, "James shows a special talent for traditional romance," and *RT Book Reviews* claims, "James deftly combines romance and suspense." Maddie is the award-winning author of over fifty titles of fiction—from short stories to novels—and a Top 100 Amazon Bestselling Author.

Learn more at www.maddiejamesbooks.com